A Dog Named Speed

A Story of Unconditional Love and Faith

Larry Fitzgerald

Published by hope*books
2217 Matthews Township Pkwy
Suite D302
Matthews, NC 28105
www.hopebooks.com

hope*books is a division of hope*media network

Printed in the United States of America by hope*books

First paperback edition.
Paperback ISBN: 979-8-89185-010-1
Hardcover ISBN: 979-8-89185-016-3
Ebook ISBN: 979-8-89185-011-8
Library of Congress Number: 2023920188

Cover image generated by Midjourney AI

All Bible references use King James Version of the Bible Modern English Version unless otherwise stated.

Table of Contents

CHAPTER 1: A STRAY DOG.................................... 1

CHAPTER 2: TEAMMATES 15

CHAPTER 3: ON MY OWN AGAIN...................... 31

CHAPTER 4: BABE 39

CHAPTER 5: A LOOK BACK 61

CHAPTER 6: PROMOTION.................................. 71

CHAPTER 7: KILROY 77

CHAPTER 8: IT TOOK FOREVER......................... 89

CHAPTER 9: THAT SOW WAS HOT 99

CHAPTER 10: YEARBOOK FIASCO 115

CHAPTER 11: DUMP REVISITED 125

CHAPTER 12: HEAD OVER HEELS 139

CHAPTER 13: FAMILY MATTERS 149

CHAPTER 14: PARTING WAYS 165

CHAPTER 15: HE'S JUST A DOG, AFTER ALL........ 183

CHAPTER 16: TIME OUT.................................... 193

CHAPTER 17: A NEW ADDRESS 205

CHAPTER 18: GOING HOME................................ 213

EPILOGUE 221

CHAPTER 1
A STRAY DOG

My name is Speed. I am a dog. Well, I was a dog when I was living on Earth. But now, I'm in heaven. I've been here since 1953. *A Dog Named Speed* is my story, based on actual events. It began when I was a pup, living between two beautiful mountain ranges in northeastern Oregon near Barrymore, a town of around eighteen hundred folks. In those early days, I had no master. I was an eight-month-old stray when I wandered into Barrymore, having jumped from the back of a pickup truck onto a highway near a mountain's summit.

My life as a stray dog wasn't easy. Most humans want nothing to do with wandering animals. We are often cruelly referred to as mongrels, curs, or mutts. I was a farm collie, a breed known for its keen intelligence, but it was clear from the beginning that no one wanted me around.

Why did people throw rocks at me or shoo me away whenever I came onto their property with a "Get out of here, you stupid mutt"? I got hit more than once. It hurt. Eventually, I just ran away when a human came close to me. My heart would pound, and my immediate instinct told me to RUN! It was safer that way. Treatment like that gave me a strong dislike for humans. Over time, the dislike turned into hate.

My stomach was always empty in those days. Often, I had no energy to even look for something to eat. Over time, I learned I could sneak up to a house where a pet lived and hijack his food, which consisted of dinky leftovers or store-bought dog or cat food most of the time. It didn't matter what it was; I gobbled down whatever was in the doggy dish and ran.

Eventually, I found another place to eat—the city dump. There was always a variety of things to eat there, and some of them tasted good. But I never spent much time tasting. I just ate as fast as I could and skedaddled. I had to eat-and-run because a caretaker lived in a trailer on the edge of the dump, and he was mean. I was afraid of him. He carried a device that made loud, popping noises. When this human drank alcohol, he would step outside the trailer house, often with a little dog at his side, and cause this device to go *pop, pop, pop*. It scared me. He would laugh and carry on, running back and forth on his porch and acting crazy. I hated him.

I guess he got away with this because he didn't have neighbors. His dog, which looked to be a mix between a Pekingese and a Chihuahua, would run back and forth, barking his head off. The porch was gated, so I knew I would not have to contend with the little guy off the porch. The caretaker was scary, so I kept one eye on the porch and the other on the food. I always had to dine and dash when I ate at the city dump.

My other challenge was to find a place I could settle into and call home. After several days of exploring, I found it. It was perfect. South of town, there was a hill called Hogsback, a long, narrow hill with several scrub pine trees which was a home for many of God's creatures. Small caves carved into the hillside were available and out of the weather. Most were shallow and dry and would be protective in the winter and shady and cool in the summer.

After weeks of living alone on Hogsback, I met a dog I named Big. Now, Big and I did not get off to an ideal start with one another. I came home to my cave late one afternoon, and as I entered, I found myself face to face with a mountain of a dog. I was unsure of his ancestry, but he was likely a terrier and maybe some mountain dog mix. He was older than I was.

I became furious as I studied this intruder who had crashed into my house! Of course, the main question was why he was even here. I could feel the fur on the back of my neck rising as I looked him straight in the eye, and with my meanest growl, I snarled "GET OUT OF HERE, NOW!!"

He returned my angry growl by casually grunting, "Buzz off, squirt," as he began to move around in a circle as dogs sometimes do before we lie down. I was hot! This uninvited guest didn't care about me; he just wanted a place to crash and chose my home.

I lost my temper and good sense at this mutt's disrespect and attacked with the vicious intent of ripping his ears off and stuffing them down his throat, after which I would eject him from my cave.

"Get out of my house," I barked, launching into him with bared fangs and an intent to kill. A wise and experienced warrior who was not surprised by my charge, Big planted his feet, caught me in mid-air, grabbed me by my neck, and threw me to the ground. In the flash of a millisecond, I was on my back, looking up at two enormous rows of gleaming white teeth backed up by a pair of intense and piercing black eyes.

"Don't mess with me, Junior."

After a few fearful minutes, Big moved away and found a comfortable spot to lie down. That is where he spent the night. He knew he was unwanted and uninvited but couldn't care less.

Following our battle, I endured a sleepless night, lifting my head often to see if Big was still around. Unfortunately, he was there every time I looked, which made me feel sick to my stomach. After several restless hours, I got up and left the cave, hoping Big would vacate the premises before I returned.

I was in a bitter mood as I made my way down the side of Hogsback that morning. As I distanced myself from my home, I began to think it might be a good time to look for a new home, something further south— perhaps something on the other side of the lumber mill which bordered Hogsback's entire south side. I had never explored that area, which was mainly foothill country with prairie grass and colossal rock formations along the east side of a steep mountain range. There should be several cave enclosures running along the base of the mountain. Excitement surged within me as I considered this new and unexplored territory's possibilities.

The landscape was beautiful and inviting. As I made my way south, I felt a light morning chill. The mountain breeze brought me pleasant smells of fresh pine needles, wildflowers, and barn and animal odors from the farms that populated the mountain base. The tantalizing aromas of breakfasts cooking in some of the farmhouses caused me to make a mental note to come back and revisit these homes sometime soon.

As I trotted along, I noticed a wide ravine to my right, which seemed popular with the birds. A bubbling stream of water flowing downhill looked appealing to a now-thirsty wanderer who had been on the go since early morning. I liked the area. It was close to town and would allow me to continue my regular dining routine. Encouraged, I turned west and headed up the ravine. I was now super excited and reenergized.

Before long, the sun was up, and I welcomed the warmth as I propelled myself uphill. The ground soon began to feel damp beneath my feet, so I moved to the side of the stream and took my first taste of the snowmelt descending the mountain. The water was frigid but tasted good. I took several gulps before continuing my journey.

As I advanced further into the ravine, the sun began to play peek-a-boo with me as I entered the mountainside's dark shadows. Doggedly determined to find a new home, I explored the entire length of the ravine and all the possible homesites it offered. But after a long time of intense searching, I concluded nothing was suitable in the area, so I reluctantly turned back to look elsewhere.

While retracing my way back downstream, I began to question myself. *Why am I doing this? I have a great home that is worth defending. Big has no right to be there. That mutt should be the one looking for new digs, not me.* The answer became obvious. I needed to return to my cave and kick that stupid mutt out of my house. So what if Big was as big as a horse? The property belonged to me, and it was worth fighting for. Big had to go. IT WAS OVER! One of us would be gone by nightfall, and IT WOULD NOT BE ME!

I felt much better and was gliding along quite smartly now, confident I would resolve my problem with Big shortly. This obnoxious freeloader would be gone by sundown, and life would be perfect again.

Patches of morning fog blanketed much of the area I passed through. The mist did not bother me because I was merely retracing my tracks from my earlier ascent up the ravine. But suddenly, I came upon several animal tracks that were new and fresh. These tracks caused me concern, so I slowed down. My olfactory senses leaped into action. The smell and my intuition warned that danger lay ahead. My pace slowed, and I cautiously moved forward, pausing several times to listen for trouble—and indeed, the problem showed up. In a few minutes, I was face to face with a pack of lean and mean-looking dog-like animals. Things got spooky as these animals slinked toward me, snarling and drooling with apparent intentions to surround me and rip me to shreds.

I had never seen animals like these. They looked like dogs, but they were all colorless and carbon copies of one another. What were they? I know now, of course; they were a pack of coyotes. And they had a thirst for blood—my blood. My heart began to pound as they moved toward me. Then, as if by some silent signal, four of them split off, attempting to get on either side of me and block me from any escape. It was likely they had done this many times. They began to vent blood-piercing shrieks and close in around me. I retaliated with fierce, loud barking as I backed up to the nearest tree—a weak response, but all I had.

Suddenly, they came. One of the animals charged and lashed at me, opening a gash on my left back flank. The next minute, I was one-on-one with their apparent leader, going by his ferocity and the many scars he carried on his muzzle and neck. He let out a sharp, piercing howl, signaling to the rest of the pack that the battle was on. He came at me full force, and as he lunged, I caught him by his neck and sank my teeth deep into his throat. I knew he was hurt because he wailed loudly and turned to the side, a momentary victory at best. My counterpunch enraged the attackers, and they immediately charged.

It was soon apparent I had no chance of winning this battle. The odds were clearly against me. However, I was determined not to go down without a fight. With my back against the tree, I fought hard, returning bite for bite, slash for slash. But I soon felt overwhelmed and overpowered. Though bleeding profusely from the many wounds inflicted by these animals, I continued to fight back, pivoting and squirming, planting my feet to absorb their attacks and then driving forward when the opportunities presented themselves. I tried to avoid getting too far from the tree, which protected me from the back. They kept coming at me, darting in and out, grabbing any part of me they could seize and rip away flesh and fur. Bleeding and gasping for air, I knew it would soon be over. I had no chance.

But miraculously, at that moment, the situation took an extraordinary turn. Suddenly, out of the cover of the low-hanging fog a thunderous burst of brown and white four-legged power named Big emerged, plowing through the entire pack and throwing animals left and right. These poor coyotes didn't know what hit them. They scattered, bleeding and limping from a very short fight. Big instantly overpowered the whole pack. They had no answer for him. They were gone in moments, having escaped into the heavy brush bordering the ravine. Big and I quickly departed, leaving the beaten and whimpering animals behind to nurse their wounds.

In those few minutes, Big went from being my worst enemy to my best friend. How amazing was that? At the time, I had no idea how or why Big showed up to save me. Maybe it was because he heard all the commotion and recognized I was in trouble. But I know that God sent him. There was no other answer. He told Big I was in trouble and put him on my scent.

With that pivotal event, of course, everything changed. Big established himself as my permanent cave-mate and had unquestioned rights wherever he wanted to lay his head. I now had a friend, a close friend. I grew to love Big. He was unique and became incredibly close to me. I had never loved another being before. This experience was priceless.

Big probably accepted me because of my youth. I posed no threat to him as a rival. Also, he was lonely and needed a friend. Big was kind enough to be a big brother to me, and he was willing to teach me how to meet the challenges of living independently. We became inseparable friends. I learned a lot from Big when we roamed at night, looking for something to eat. He had a handle on where, what, and when pet owners fed their animals so we could execute our foraging to our best advantage.

Most of the food put out by pet owners went uneaten because the pets were not especially hungry or did not care for the offering. Big and I, on the other hand, were not particular. We emptied any dog dish in the neighborhood that "Fido" had not cleaned up by midnight. We would roam from yard to yard, unashamedly helping ourselves to whatever was available. It was easy because Big never cared who owned the dog dish and always made me handle the problem if the pet fussed at us. "Take your complaint to my sidekick here" was his answer to any opposition. I did my part to carry out the threat by growling and baring my fangs, and that usually took care of the matter, especially with Big standing guard nearby.

We had to step up and occasionally fight, which sometimes took place over a meal or a territory dispute. Big handled all the heavy fights when they came up, and our dog community soon learned not to mess with him.

One night, we ventured into town hungry and looking for a good meal. We caught the scent of food from the back of a small apartment building, so we headed that way.

Once we got there, two rangy and ragged-looking dogs sneered at us momentarily as they looked up from a meal they were sharing from a garbage can. They growled at us menacingly, then returned to their dinners. Still, they watched us closely. It was dark and therefore difficult to tell what they were, but they were large, probably with some terrier and German Shepherd blood in the mix. They were mean-looking and showed no intention of sharing their meal with the two of us.

In no time, Big was engaged in battle with the larger of the two. The other guy looked me over, growled several times, and then joined his partner in trying to bring Big down. I took this as an insult, and I knew two-on-one was not a fair fight, so I jumped into the middle of the action.

I had never been in a real dog fight before, other than my encounter with the coyotes—but that was not a dog fight so much as a massacre. This engagement was a bona fide dog fight—a fair fight, a may-the-best-dog-win kind of fight. Fortunately for me, the best dog was on my side. But either way, I was in the middle of this one before I had a chance to consider my options.

We got after it, standing on our back legs and slashing throats, ears, and shoulders. It didn't last very long because we were making so much noise that some humans came out of their apartments and began to scream at us. They were pretty upset.

"Get out of here," one man wailed as he picked up a brick and threw it toward us. Fortunately, his aim was off-target, and the brick sailed past us. We didn't care what those people thought. We were engaged in battle.

Several minutes of fighting went by before I felt a blast of cold water slam into my body.

"Oh yeah, that's it," a voice boomed. "Soak them good! Get out of here. Scram, you stupid mutts."

Big decided it was time to leave, so we grabbed the remaining food and took off for home. We were cold and wet, but we managed to shake most of the water away by the time we returned to Hogsback, where we quietly finished our meal.

It had been an exciting night. We felt good, and I learned some dogfighting techniques, which would serve me well over the coming years. Of course, this was routine for Big. However, I could sense his approval as he paused his eating and looked at me for several seconds before returning to his dinner. We laid close together that night, two warriors who experienced the thrill of victory and the rewards of an excellent meal. We even had some bones left over to chew on the next day.

Word must have gotten around about Big and me because all the dogs in town began to cut us a wide swath after that. Of course, they respected Big more than me, but that didn't bother me. I knew if I were with Big, I would get some respect just from being his friend—and he was a good friend. Life was simple for the two of us. Our days consisted of lazing around our cave and foraging for food at night. We were living a good life, but that was about to change.

CHAPTER 2
TEAMMATES

Big didn't trust humans any more than I did. He hated their smell and could tell a human being was around even when none were close. He had good reason. As a pup, Big was inhumanely tossed into a nest of wasps by two thrill-seeking young men and stung repeatedly. His spontaneous reactions to the constant stinging brought a shameful burst of hilarity to the mean people who were amused by his bodily responses. Soon after that, some humans put Big and his brothers and sisters in a large bag and dumped them into a river. Big was the only survivor. He had pulled himself onto a small clump of brush lodged at the end of a beaver dam.

After that, Big was on his own. However, he had to endure being picked up more than once by animal control. He was adopted each time but did not stick around with new owners long enough to allow relationships to develop. Every time he had the chance to escape, he seized the opportunity. I could understand. I would have done the same thing if it had been me. Both of us wanted nothing to do with humans. So, as it turned out, I was the only family Big knew. And Big was the only family I knew. No problem. We were good with that.

The weather was sub-freezing the first winter we were together. We went to sleep each night huddled together to stay warm. Inside the cave, we dug out a large but shallow hole, which became our bed. The winter that year was a record-breaker for snowfall. Morning after morning, we had to break through big snowdrifts that homed in on our hillside, covering the entrances to the caves. I didn't mind the snow all that much, but Big had difficulty making his way around because he was so heavy. He sank chest-deep with every step he took. I usually managed to stay on top of the snow and got around easier than Big.

Besides scavenging meals at the city dump and from the dishes of all the domestic pets in town, Big had another arrow in his quiver, one I had never considered. Barrymore was a small town with close to eighteen hundred residents. Nestled down at the north end of an expansive and vibrant valley, it cast an impression of peace and serenity, an ideal place to live. Folks moved there, and the town grew.

People built new homes. There was a new fire station, a new church on Main Street, and a new high school on the southwest side of town. And, of course, new construction meant engineers, carpenters, bricklayers, landscapers, and plumbers. Many workers walked to work because of Barrymore's small size, carrying their lunches in paper bags. The worker would leave his lunch unsecured in an open area, inside a building under construction, on an unfinished windowsill, or inside an unfinished doorway. Because we could pick up scents, these lunch bags were no problem for Big and me to locate.

You get the picture. Big and I would pull off quick raids, hitting a new building site to grab an unguarded lunch sack and scrambling for cover before anyone noticed. These meals were always fine, except when pickles or onions were part of the package. Everything else was acceptable, even lettuce and carrots. To a hungry dog, it was all good. The gig was almost foolproof, and we got to the point where we were so confident in this part of our playbook that we began to get careless, or maybe you could label it reckless bravado. The inevitable happened. I got caught.

Big and I strutted into a neighborhood where a few new homes were under construction on one warm August morning. Easy targets! Big went for one of the new homes and I went to another, each of us attracted by the alluring aromas of tuna and bologna sandwiches wafting from the new buildings. Big was in and out of his building in less than ten seconds, a bagged lunch between his jaws.

I was not so fortunate. The only lunch that came into view in my building was inside a lunch pail sitting on a makeshift worktable. I should have passed and moved on to the next building. But the growl in my stomach wouldn't let me. Without hesitation, I stood on my hind legs and tried to grab the handle of the lunch pail. That didn't work, and the gig was over in less than a minute. I felt a sudden tug on the rope attached to the collar that had hung around my neck for several months, a leftover from my previous owner. The man who owned the lunch had a grip on the other end.

"No, you don't, pooch," he uttered as he pulled me away from his lunch bucket. "That's my lunch you're messing with."

I squirmed and dug my feet into the unfinished floor, pulling away from my captor as best I could. In just a few seconds, a second human came over to us. He said, "That's one of the lunch bandits. It looks like we finally caught one. Nice going."

"So, what do we do with him?"

The second man shrugged his shoulders. "Take him out and shoot him, as far as I'm concerned. I doubt he belongs to anyone."

"Yeah, except he has a collar on," the man holding me said. "He must belong to someone. Or he used to, anyway."

Of course, I did not know what these men were saying to one another. I was only reminded of my hatred for humans as the man jerked me around by my collar, trying to get a closer look. I resisted, straining against the rope. Fortunately for me, at that moment, the collar, badly weakened by age, broke and fell off in the man's hand. Feeling the sudden loss of restraint, I bolted. The man grabbed at me, but he had no chance. I broke away from him and blew out of the building. I rejoiced over my narrow escape as I ran back toward my home on Hogsback. I felt strong as I ran, knowing no human could control me. I was free! I was alive! And I hated humans even more, because every one of them wanted to steal my freedom.

I knew Big would be waiting for me somewhere along the way back to our home on Hogsback. I found him near a high school under construction that was south of town. He was lying down in the shade of a lonely scrub pine tree which was sure to become the victim of a chainsaw soon because, unfortunately for the tree, it was in the middle of a future baseball field.

"Where you been?" Big snorted.

Let me assure you, Big and I were best friends. There was no doubt about that. However, he did not wait for me to eat his lunch. He quickly consumed the tasty stuff; the only food left was an apple. Big pushed the apple over to me with his nose.

"I don't like apples," he growled.

I liked apples, so I grabbed it as it rolled my way and gobbled it down before Big could change his mind.

We spent a few lazy hours lying under the tree and enjoying the afternoon sunshine. When the sun began to disappear behind the beautiful mountain range, we got to our feet and trotted to our home on Hogsback. It had been an interesting and exciting day, even though my supper had been one meager apple.

Big and I continued working the neighborhoods, including the new construction areas. We were more cautious now when raiding construction sites, however. We stayed out of sight as best we could and ensured no humans were nearby before we charged in and grabbed lunch. If there were any signs of danger, we let the opportunity pass. The extra caution paid off, as we never had another close call.

I understand now that it was wrong to steal the workers' lunches. That was stealing, and the Bible has plenty to say about that. We were taking something that was not ours and shouldn't have done that. But please remember, God has not set the high standard for animals that He has for humans. Humans are born with consciences, and if they do something their conscience tells them not to do, most of the time, it's a sin. Animals are not born with a conscience. It was not until I got to heaven that I learned that. One of the best things about heaven is that there is no sin here. Heaven is perfect. God's glory lives here. The Bible says people have no idea what heaven is like and will be amazed to see what God has prepared for the ones who come here.

There is no sadness in heaven, for God has wiped every tear from the eyes of those here. From my current vantage point, I can attest to the goodness here. Heaven is a true paradise. It makes me very sad when I think of the many who live on Earth and will never see the heaven where I live because they have never invited God to be a part of their lives.

* * *

One afternoon, Big and I decided we needed a change in scenery for our evening dinner. I'm unsure why. Maybe it was because we were tired of store-bought dog food and leftovers. Our construction site forays were becoming less fruitful. The workers had heard about us and took precautions to protect their lunches. They began stashing them in storage lockers or up high in a building where we couldn't reach them. Whatever the reason, we decided to head to the city refuse dump. The dump was often a good idea because there was always variety, but you had to be willing to move around and avoid the caretaker. We knew there was some risk, but it would be dark soon, so we thought we would be all right.

It was dusk when we reached the outer edge of the dump. I figured we would split up and forage for food alone, but that wasn't what Big wanted to do. He decided we should stick together, so we worked side by side, poking our noses into open sacks and containers strewn about in every way imaginable by workers, other animals, and, occasionally, high winds that blew through the area. Much of the dump was smoldering from a recent burn, so we stayed away from those areas. We also had to avoid the many shards of broken glass scattered around the city dump.

As luck would have it, we soon came upon a large box filled with bags of goodies, including Big hush puppies and chicken scraps, probably leftovers from a family picnic. We stopped, and I began to eat my dinner. I noticed, however, that Big seemed more interested in watching for danger signs than he did in eating. He kept looking up and searching for any unwelcome scent or indication of danger. Me, I wasn't worried. I was hungry.

Big was right to be careful. Suddenly, we heard that familiar popping noise again, followed by pinging sounds close to us. I was slow to catch on to what was happening, but Big sure wasn't. Our eyes locked briefly as his neck and back fur stood straight up. That scared me for sure. I started to stand up, but Big stayed low and gave me a nasty snarl.

"Stay here and stay down," he growled.

He suddenly took off, running away from the scene fast. My heart began to race when I heard him crashing through trash and junk. I stayed where I was, out of sight as Big had directed me. I was unsure how, but Big quickly succeeded in getting several yards away from me, disappearing and reappearing in and out of the jumbled-up mayhem of the city dump. I just crouched down in place for several anxious minutes. I wanted to work my way over to where I had last seen Big but thought better of it. Such a move might endanger him. Then I thought about breaking away in the opposite direction from Big. That would divert attention to me and give Big the best chance of escaping. So, I gathered myself into a tense springing position, ready to launch, until I heard more popping sounds. I held back. Everything grew silent.

A light breeze began to whisper through the junkyard. Loose sandwich wrappers drifted back and forth. I kept my head down. What was going on? Suddenly, I heard someone running to my right, toward where I had last seen Big. I had to sneak a look. When I did, I saw a clear view of the caretaker running away from me. I watched him run for several minutes before he came to an abrupt stop. At once, there was a sudden eruption out of his rifle. I watched the caretaker slowly lower his weapon and stare at the rubble ahead. Then he swung his head around, likely looking for something else to shoot. I ducked my head back down and didn't move, fearing he would see me. Thankfully, he didn't. After a few moments, I heard him vent a sinister chuckle and stumble away through the garbage and back toward his trailer.

When I was sure the caretaker was gone, I slowly raised myself and went to where he had been standing, afraid of what I might see. I saw Big stretched out and lying very still when I reached the spot where he had fallen. I crept over to where he lay and touched him with my nose. Blood gurgled from the wounds in his side. Big was severely hurt, and I felt sick and weak. My heart began to pound in my chest. My whole body was shaking.

"Big. Are you alright?" I whined, knowing full well that he wasn't.

Big slowly raised his head and looked up at me. I knew he had to be in great pain, but to my surprise, his look was not of pain, but of love. Big was telling me goodbye.

"You're on your own now, kid. Take care of yourself. I love you, pal."

He laid his head down and closed his eyes. I crawled to him, touched his head with my nose, and tenderly licked his face. I lay there with my nose on his muzzle for a long time, hoping my friend would start breathing and jump up so we could take off together to our home on the hill.

"Big, wake up. We need to get out of here. Big, do you hear me?"

But all I could hear was my heart pounding, my own pathetic whining, and the papers fluttering around me. Big didn't move. I had no control over my sickening feeling that bordered on panic, and I had no control over my whining. It was as if I were outside my body, watching a painful episode where I could do nothing.

By contrast, Big just lay there, looking very peaceful. I nudged him with my nose and continued to lick his face. It was total instinct. He didn't move, and he wasn't breathing. My best and only friend in the world was lifeless. I had never seen death before, and I was helpless.

Suddenly, the moment's serenity was cruelly interrupted by an unbelievable scene on the caretaker's porch. I saw the man stumbling around and singing, causing me to hunker down out of sight again. He couldn't see me, but even if he could have, it would not have done him any good, because he was drunk and out of control. He cradled his little dog and a bottle in his arms, a proud and heartless human being.

How can a man shoot and kill an innocent animal, then celebrate the occasion by holding his own animal in his arms as a protective master, singing his foolish head off out of sheer glee? I hate humans!

As the evening skies grew dark, I knew it was safe to stay with Big. And as I think today about my friend's grave in a city refuse dump, I know that soon, he would have been covered up with the next week's garbage and eventually burned up along with the rest of the refuse.

It was a sad and humble ending, even for a dog—but a beloved dog. He deserved better. Looking at Big, I could not help but think how unfair life was. A human had taken me from my real family, and after experiencing cruel treatment by evil men, I had managed to escape into a life of my own. And how perfect things had been after Big came along! Now, Big was dead, killed by a man who had no idea what he was doing. He just liked to kill things. How sad. As for Big, it was a tragic ending for his incredibly free spirit.

After lying there for some time, I became aware of a large bird passing just a few dozen feet above my head before soaring toward a lonely pine tree up on the eastern edge of the dump. The tree had, by some miracle, managed to survive in this toxic environment. The bird landed on one of the bare limbs protruding from the tree trunk. This scene was strangely familiar because I knew I had seen that bird make that same landing a year or more ago when I first came to my new home in Barrymore. I immediately recognized my friend, who I had named "Hootie" the day we first met.

The majestic owl looked at me and hooted, "Hello friend."

Hootie and I gazed at one another for several minutes. Finally, I stood and stumbled my way around the piled-up debris to the base of the tree on which Hootie was perched. I put my front feet on the trunk, just as before. He hooted again and blinked those huge eyes at me.

"Why such a sad look, my friend?"

"My best friend has just been killed, Hootie."

"I am so sorry to hear that. Are you okay?"

"Not until I get even."

"Never pay back evil for evil, my friend."

"You don't understand, Hootie. A very bad man just killed my best friend. I hate him."

"Let it be, collie dog. Let it be. Hatred destroys. Learn to love."

As Hootie sat on the limb and peered down at me, I respected his wisdom and assurance, but this was different. He didn't understand. In a few minutes, he launched into the air, soared high into the moonlit sky, and disappeared.

I spent that night with Big, and when the morning sunlight broke over the eastern skyline, I looked at my friend and said goodbye to him. As I stood, I locked my gaze on the home of my great enemy. It was odd because sunlight surrounded the mobile home, but the trailer was dark. I swore to myself that no matter how long it took, I would get even with the man who had killed my best friend. He would pay. And he would pay dearly!

Then, I charged the trailer house at full speed in an out-of-control burst of anger—a proper ending to an emotion-filled night. When I got to the front porch, I shrieked out my hatred at the top of my voice. In a moment, every light inside the house came on. I could hear the people inside come alive with angry voices. That did not deter me. Suddenly, the door swung open, and the half-dressed caretaker appeared. As soon as he saw me, he quickly disappeared back inside. I knew what that meant, so I hightailed it out of there, not wanting to let this killer have the satisfaction of claiming his second victim so soon after his first. As I left the dump behind, I knew I would be back one day and not for the pleasure of a meal.

In my cave that night, my entire body ached with hatred and hostility toward everything human. It ate away at me and compounded my fear of all human beings. I was determined never to go near or have anything to do with human beings, EVER!

CHAPTER 3
ON MY OWN AGAIN

To say Big had influenced me would be an understatement. Because of his strong personality and character, my self-confidence blossomed. I became more adventurous and willing to assert myself with other animals. I mimicked Big's swagger, and other dogs challenged me. By necessity, I honed my fighting skills and soon had a reputation as a canine not to test. Life became simple again. I would start each day with an early search for food, stroll through town with a purpose, avoid trouble, stay away from humans, and avoid going near the city dump. I also found it beneficial to make enlarged circuits when I looked for food.

One winter day, I found myself heading away from town with a couple of companions. These guys were not exactly friends. We just happened to frequent many of the same places daily as we scavenged for food.

We headed south out of town on a railway bed. None of us knew where we were going, nor did we care. We just got caught up in the desire to explore, to see something different. We came upon a small sawmill about three miles from town. It seemed deserted, meaning we saw no humans there. There were huge piles of logs stacked neatly alongside a frozen pond. Several ducks flew over, close to the iced-over pond. I was not a bird dog by breed, but the other guys must have been because they made a beeline to the pond's edge and started barking at these birds. The ducks responded by flying away momentarily, assuming a wide arc and circling back over the pond at a slightly higher elevation. I joined the game, barking like crazy as I rushed to the pond.

That was a mistake because I didn't stop at the pond's edge and continued running out onto the ice, an unfortunate decision. Several yards out, I hit a thin spot in the ice and soon found myself thrashing around in the water, which was freezing. I was in trouble. I paddled around, trying to scramble out of the water by pulling myself up on the ice's edge, a useless waste of energy. Every time I got a forepaw on the ice shelf's edge, the ice broke off, and I would be back in the water. My predicament went on for a tortuously long time, and I soon reached the point of exhaustion. My companions were wiser than me and had remained on shore. They milled around and watched me for a while as I struggled to get out of the water, but they soon became uninterested and wandered away, back toward town. Their fickleness didn't bother me as much as my plight, which grew steadily worse as I struggled to get out of the water. My fur coat became water-logged and heavy like an anchor weighing me down.

I grew fearful, which made matters worse, and I started running out of air as I struggled to get back onto the ice. Nothing worked. Soon, I was exhausted, barely able to keep my head above water. Fear turned to panic as I sank deeper into the water. My lungs began to fill with water, so I attempted one final effort to get back to the surface. When my head popped up, I desperately tried to get my legs up on the ice, which I somehow managed to do, but my body was too heavy. I didn't have enough strength to pull myself onto the ice. I knew it was over then and stopped struggling. I lost the battle and began to sink. A strange calm came over me. I started to lose consciousness and descend downward. It was over.

But at that moment, an even stranger thing happened. I felt a strong force encircle my body and lift me up and out of the water. With the aid of this force, I was placed on the ice and forcefully scooted toward the shore. Something lifted me and set me on the beach at the pond's edge. I didn't know what was happening, as

I was primarily unconscious while all of this happened. I vaguely remember lying on the ground, feeling intermittent pressure on my sides and water gurgling out of my mouth. Someone or something was blowing refreshing gulps of air into my mouth.

I was confused but glad to be out of the water and lying on solid ground. I have no idea how long the rescue attempt went on, but as my instincts returned, I realized those attending to me were humans, and I hated humans. Even though I was happy with what they did, I wanted nothing to do with them. Their smell repelled me, and I needed to get away from them. So, I lay there quietly, hoping I would be strong enough when the opportunity came for me to grab my chance to bolt away.

Meanwhile, the two men were attentive. They covered me with a blanket and occasionally gave me a pat or two on my head. I couldn't understand this, but my instincts were screaming, "You need to leave!" I knew that, but I quickly realized there was no bolt in me when I tried to get up. My legs wobbled. I couldn't even manage a weak crawl, for that matter. So, I just lay back down on the blanket. In the background, over the relentless wake of the waves splashing against the shoreline, I could hear the men talking, no doubt about me.

"You know," said Man Number One. "I may be crazy, but I recognize this dog."

"How so?" asked Man Number Two.

"I swear he is one of the dogs who was stealing our lunches last summer when we were working on the Latimer project. He sure looks like him, anyway."

"That's interesting."

"I know. There were two dogs. I saw them more than once. They would dart in, grab a lunch bag, and be gone before we knew they had even been there."

Man Number Two chuckled and said, "Sounds like a couple of smart dogs. Did either one of them ever get your lunch?"

"Not him, I don't think. But I know his partner did once. I could have killed him!"

Man Number Two walked over and stood over me.

"He looks pretty innocent right now," he said. "Are you going to take him home?"

"I don't know. I might. Why don't you take him home? He'd make you a good dog, maybe."

"Nope. I have two dogs now. Besides, how do we know this guy doesn't belong to somebody?"

"I doubt if anyone owns this sorry-looking mess of a dog."

"Then do it, man! Take him home with you tonight after we finish this job."

Both men stared at me in silence for a long time. I had no idea what they had been saying, but I was sure they were talking about me. They may have been plans for me, but despite their heroics in rescuing me, I had no plans for them.

Finally, Man Number One said, "I'll tell you what. Let's leave the dog here and finish our job. I'll take him home when we're ready to leave if he's still here. If he's not, so be it."

"Are you sure you don't want to put a rope on him and tie him to that tree? Otherwise, I doubt he will stick around once we leave."

Man Number One paused again before answering, "No, I don't think so. If I tried that, he might go crazy, which could cause him to hurt himself. If God wants me to have this dog, He will see to it. If not, the dog will belong to someone else. I'm fine with that."

* * *

I'm not sure how much longer I lay there. I heard the men drive away in their truck. I was aware of the afternoon sun warming my body, and it felt good. I was tired and must have gone to sleep for a while. Finally, I raised my head and looked around. No one was there.

It was quiet and peaceful except for the ducks coming and going. I wondered where the men who had pulled me out of the water were. Or had that been a dream?

It must have been a dream, because no human has ever done anything but hurt me in my whole life.

I hated humans, and the smell of them was all around me. I needed to leave, so I struggled to get up. I found it difficult and painful, but I could steady myself and look around once I was on all fours. I became aware of half a sandwich on the blanket I had been on and made short work of that. It made me think of Big and the many lunchtimes we shared.

I sensed that the men would return. I needed to get out of there, so I left. I am very thankful for those men. I never saw them again, but I have never forgotten what they did for me. I learned a significant lesson about how precious life is and how wisdom comes from making wrong decisions. I saw how God gave me a second chance at life through two strange men demonstrating how love can overcome hate.

Over the next few weeks, life returned to normal. However, finding food, staying warm, and defending my territory were still challenges. I also found myself more curious about humans than I had ever been. Yes, they still chased me off their properties at times, but I began to have a new sense of curiosity about them. And it bothered me a lot that two humans had saved me from drowning while my kind deserted me. So, I was confused but remained distrustful of anyone who walked on two legs. I maintained a safe distance from any human who came near me. I refused to drop my guard.

And that's how things remained until I met a newspaper boy.

CHAPTER 4
BABE

Babe was a twelve-year-old boy who delivered newspapers in Barrymore and the surrounding area. I would see him early every morning carrying a large bag of newspapers strapped to his shoulders. He would ride his bicycle up to a house, throw a paper on the front porch, and then pedal off to the next subscriber on his route. Because of my newfound curiosity about humans, I began to follow him from a distance, and whenever he saw me, he stopped his bicycle and whistled at me, pounding on his knee. He always smiled at me and enthusiastically coaxed me to come closer.

He would say, "Here, boy. Come on. Nobody's going to hurt you."

I didn't know if it was his enthusiasm or youthfulness, but he seemed much different from other humans I had been around. Babe was a spark of energy, always smiling and encouraging me to come to him. It was tempting, but

I never took the bait. This boy had too good a throwing arm, and I didn't want to take a chance of getting hit by a rock or a rolled-up newspaper. Besides that, he was a human, so I didn't trust him.

However, I continued to tag along from a safe distance every morning, probably because we were the only ones out then. I never took the young man up on his offer of friendship. I continued to follow him at a distance, basically because I had nothing else to do.

Each morning, his last stop was a white house with a large front porch. He would store his bike in an unattached garage, walk up the steps, and disappear inside. I always hung back, a block or two away. Whenever he saw me, however, instead of going inside the house, he would come back off the porch, walk down the steps, and try to coax me forward. But I wouldn't fall for it. No way! My tail would automatically drop between my legs, and if he started to walk toward me, I was out of there like a speeding bullet.

* * *

It would be a lie to say life had any meaning for me in the days following Big's death. He had been a friend like no other. My life was empty, dull, and sad. I knew I would never have another friend like Big, nor did I want one. What I was going through was not something

I would ever care to experience again. Why would I ever wish for another friend anyway? No creature could ever measure up to Big!

But I was very lonesome. Nights were endless, and other than the drudgery of looking for something to eat, the days were not any better. I returned to my cave home on Hogsback each night and waited for morning to come so I could start the grind all over again.

Occasionally, a strange animal would appear at my cave entrance and curiously look inside. Sometimes, an opossum would stick its furry little head in and sniff around. I had nothing against opossums and would usually wag my tail in friendship, but they never saw it that way and made rapid retreats. There was a bobcat who showed up occasionally, but all it took was a low growl or two from me, and the would-be visitor would be on his way. It wasn't personal. There was just something about cats I instinctively didn't like.

The lumber mill behind Hogsback would trigger a howling siren at seven o'clock every morning, and it always woke me up. Fortunately, the siren only wailed for a minute or two, which was good because it was so loud and close that it hurt my ears. I would wake up, stretch, yawn, scratch where I itched, and head out for breakfast.

When I look back on those days, except for the loneliness of life without Big, I had nothing to complain about. Cold nights bothered me more now that Big was no longer there to curl around. Some nights were more brutal than others, of course, and I was always happy when daytime came, when the sun popped out and warmed things up.

But there was one night that got so frigid my fur coat could not keep me warm. I couldn't stop shaking no matter what I did, which drove me crazy. I had never been so cold or so miserable.

I lay in my cave, listening to the wind howl until I couldn't take it any longer. I left my cave and started wandering around town, hoping for warmth by moving around. I was also hungry. Most of the pet dishes were inside. Pet owners who loved their pets protected them from the cold by bringing them inside, so, there was little food and no place to escape the cold. It was dark and getting colder by the minute. I wandered the streets until I grew so tired, I could hardly drag myself forward. But I had to. Somehow, I knew it was necessary to keep moving, so that is what I did, creeping from yard to yard and street to street, hoping to find warmth. However, I found none, and I was beginning to lose hope. My senses were shutting down. Each step forward became a decision. And the streets were empty, except for me.

Eventually, and probably not by accident, my steps brought me to the front of the newspaper boy's house. Yeah, I was scared, but now I was more desperate than scared. I pulled myself onto the porch one painful step at a time and plopped down on a mat in front of the storm door, where I could feel a whisper of warmth from under the threshold.

While I lay there, pressing up to the door as close as possible, I could hear a horn playing notes of a melody inside the house. I wasn't sure what it was, but the sound was pleasant and helped me temporarily forget how miserable I was. The tones flowed at varying intensities and ranged from low to high frequencies. Finally, the pitch went so high that I felt compelled to join in. I put my nose in the air and crooned in harmony with what was coming from the house. It was a reflex. I couldn't hold it back.

At that, the music inside abruptly stopped. I could hear people stirring around. Then the house door opened, and the newspaper kid appeared. He stared at me through the storm door window. Then, still looking at me, he hollered, "Mom, come here, quick!"

The boy began to jump up and down. That scared me, so I forced myself to stand. I wanted to leave but couldn't, so I crawled to a far corner of the porch and lay on the hard wooden floor.

In short order, the boy's mom appeared at the door. She looked out on the porch and said, "What is it, Babe?"

Hopping from one foot to the other, Babe was highly excited. "It's him. The dog I told you about who has been following me on my paper route."

He pushed the door open far enough for his mom to see. I remember raising my head and wagging my tail. I was too weak to stand, but I smiled. Yes, that's correct. I smiled. In those days, whenever I felt sheepish or uncertain of myself, my lips would recede, exposing my upper front teeth. It was not a snarl, although it looked like one. It was a genuine smile, mostly because I felt insecure. I couldn't control it.

"He's cold and scared, Mom. Look at him shiver." Babe stepped out onto the porch, walked toward me, and knelt. He had no rock and no newspaper, yet I was uneasy. He was a human. I still didn't trust humans. I lowered my head between my front paws, looked up at him, and wagged my tail.

"It's okay, boy," he said, stretching his hand out for me to sniff. Then he started patting me softly on my head. "It's okay. Good boy."

He turned back toward his mom, who had stepped onto the porch and closed the storm door. The cold night air caused her to shiver and hug herself.

"He's freezing, Mom."

"He's not alone. Come back inside, Babe. It's too cold out here."

"And I bet he's hungry. Can we feed him, Mom?"

"Oh, I don't know, dear. That dog must belong to someone; the owners are probably looking for him. We'd better not, Babe."

"But Mom, he can't belong to anyone. He doesn't have a collar on, and he always follows me around on my paper route. Look at him. His coat is all dirty and full of grease and cockleburs. He is nothing but skin and bones. If somebody owned and cared about him, he wouldn't look like this."

Babe's mom muttered an impatient sigh and said, "Okay, son, I'll see what we have in the refrigerator. But do not get your hopes up. I am sure he must belong to someone."

"Do we have an old carpet or mat he could have? This floor is hard."

"Oh dear," she said, then sighed, "Well, there might be something. I'll look."

As Babe knelt beside me, gently stroking my burr-tangled and dirty fur, I felt love from a human for the first time. It was a moment I will never forget, and I didn't want it to end. He snuggled up and put his arms around my neck, pulling me close. His warm body warmed my body. I breathed in his unique body smells and felt a peace and comfort I had never known. I couldn't help it. I fell in love with Babe at that very moment.

I had a nice, warm meal that night, and I slept on a clean carpet and an old blanket Babe's mom had found in the attic. When the lights went out inside the house, I excitedly looked forward to the next day when I would see Babe again. Little did I know that Babe's final thoughts as he went to sleep that night were grave concerns that I would disappear during the night. He worried that I might return to wherever I lived before coming to his house, but that was the furthest thing from my mind. I was in an incredible place and had no plans to go anywhere.

Early the next morning, I heard the front door open and saw Babe step out on the porch. He seemed as relieved to see me as I was to see him. He grinned. I wagged my tail. Then, I cocked my head and stared at the young man as he approached me. He offered me a piece of toast, which I wasted no time gulping down. My excitement spiked with an immediate love for Babe—the kind of love I had known with Big, only different. Better! Babe knelt and slowly began to stroke the top of my head. I felt his love. It was genuine, and it felt good.

"Good boy," he said. "Did you sleep well?" Then he put his mouth next to my ear and whispered, "Don't tell anybody, but I think my parents will let me keep you. How would you like that?" I didn't understand his words, but I could tell from his excitement that they were special.

In a few minutes, another young man stepped out onto the porch. He was older and bigger than Babe. He came over and stood beside Babe.

"So, this is the mutt you want to adopt, little brother? He looks like a loser to me."

"He just needs a bath, Den. He's a beautiful dog. You'll see when I get him cleaned up."

"Well, that will have to wait, Babe. We have papers to deliver, and we need to get going."

"I know." Babe looked at me and rubbed the fur around my neck. "Are you ready to deliver some newspapers, boy?" Once again, I cocked my head and looked him in the eye. My instincts told me an adventure lay ahead. With a big grin, he stood and said, "Come on, you can come."

I was on my feet at once, prancing around and eager to go wherever Babe was. Soon, we were on our way to the train depot where the boys picked up their newspapers every morning. Of course, they were on their bikes, and I ran alongside them, proud to be an official delivery team member. Babe's route was on the north side of town and included some small outlying farmhouses on the edge of Barrymore, so we split up. Babe and I went north, and Den went south.

I can't tell you how excited I was to run ahead of Babe on this first morning of many we made over the following months delivering newspapers. Of course, I didn't know the route as well as he did, so I sometimes went to the wrong house. Not every home took the paper, which confused me early on. Babe would call out to me when it happened.

I never made that mistake twice. One time through, and I had the route down pat. Now and then, I took the opportunity to mark my new territory. This regimen is essential to us canines because it lets other animals know that a new dog is staking out claims in the neighborhood, and they had better show some respect.

Unfortunately, I did commit one major mishap that first day on the job—a rookie mistake. I'm embarrassed about it, but honesty is mandatory for residents living in heaven, and though it is embarrassing, I must include it in my story. Babe rode ahead of me as we approached the Cruikshank household and threw their paper well onto their driveway with pinpoint accuracy, just next to the walk leading down from their front porch. This placement allowed Babe's customer to retrieve it from the sidewalk easily. Babe had made this throw many times, of course.

Then, he was quickly on his way to the next house. I was determined to leave my mark at this strategic location, but I was running behind, so I marked the newly thrown newspaper out of desperation and unclear thinking. At the same time, Mr. Cruikshank opened his door to retrieve his morning paper. He caught me dead to rights. The man took an angry step towards me and expressed some unpleasant words, which I interpreted as "Get out of here." I was glad to do that, and at a high rate of speed. I shot past Babe like he was standing still. I felt terrible about the Cruikshank debacle, but fortunately, I had done so much territory marking by then that my tank was almost empty. So, no harm done, in my view, anyway.

"Hey, boy," Babe hollered at me. "Where are you going so fast?" I stopped and turned back as he caught up to me. "What's your hurry, boy? Man, you're a regular speed merchant, aren't you?" He bent down and gave me a couple of pats on my neck.

"A speedster, that's what you are. A real speedster!" He paused as he looked at me. Then he blurted out, "That's it! I'm going to name you Speedster. Or maybe just Speed. What do you think? Do you like that, boy? The name Speed." He paused for a minute, then said, "Okay then, your official name is Speed." Then Babe wrinkled his nose and added, "Man, you need a bath! You smell bad. Worse than bad. You stink." I didn't know what those words meant then, but I would soon find out.

When Babe had delivered the last paper in his bag, we circled back to the big white house. Den was already there. The boys went inside for breakfast, and Babe later brought me more toast.

"Mom's going to buy you dog food at the store today, Speed. You'll have a nice meal in a new dog dish tonight. Okay, boy?"

The boys were wearing flannel shirts, the tails of which poked out below their winter jackets. They both wore corduroy pants. And they had book bags tucked under their arms instead of newspaper bags.

Babe asked, looking at me and then his brother, "How will we keep him home while we're in school?"

"No problem. We'll just put your pup inside the garage and close the door. Dad's already gone to work. Therefore, little brother, Speed-dog will have the whole garage to himself."

"Hmm, I don't know, Den. I'm not so sure he'll like that."

"So? There's nothing he can do about it. He'll be fine. We can put his mat and water in there. He might not like it, but so what? What can he do?"

Babe gave me a few more gentle pats and a big hug. "I'll be back right after school, Speed. I promise. Good boy."

The next thing I knew, both boys were off the porch. Babe was steering me down the steps and over toward the garage door.

"Okay, Speed," Babe said. "It'll be fine. You'll be in there a few hours is all." He retrieved my mat from the porch as Den went to the garage and pulled the rope from the bottom of the garage door. With some tugging, the door slowly creaked up to where Den could push it up the rails until it was wide open. Babe steered me with his arms and legs into the garage. I was a little fearful, but Babe gave me a reassuring pat, which calmed me down. He also had another treat for me, a piece of cooked bacon, which he tossed to the front of the garage. I wondered why Babe did that as I scrambled to snag my treat. I soon found out why. Believe me, I would never fall for that trick again, that's for sure.

"Stay here, boy. I'll be back to get you after school."

Then he stepped out of the garage and quickly pulled the door back down before I knew what was happening. I soon realized I was alone in the garage. I could hear the boys' voices fade as they walked away from the building. After that, it grew eerily quiet, and I no longer had the scent of Babe and his brother in my senses.

What's going on here?

Haunting memories of being locked up in the past flooded my mind.

HOW DO I GET OUT OF HERE?

I circled the garage's interior three times, but there was no way out. My only hope was a window about three feet off the floor on one of the garage walls. I knew nothing about windows or windowpanes. All I saw was a square opening in the side of the garage with sunlight shining through that seemed to say, "Jump through here." So, I backed up and, at a dead run, launched into a flying leap and crashed through the window. My impact on the window caused an enormous explosion, with broken shards of glass flying inside and outside the garage. I hit the glass so hard it stunned me, and I fell to the ground in a heap. The broken glass landed on the ground and all over me. Dazed but not hurt, I jumped up and shook my body free of glass and wood splinters.

The boys, who had reached the large barn on the edge of the street one block from the school, heard the crash and came running back to see what had happened. When they got to me, Babe dropped to his knees and put his arms around me while Den surveyed the mess I had made.

"You okay, Speed?" Babe asked, slightly out of breath.

I didn't know what he asked, but he wasn't mad at me. I pressed into him and received a reassuring hug in return.

Babe looked at Den, "What will we tell Dad?"

"I don't know, little brother, but we're late for school. We better get going."

"What about my dog?"

"That's his problem. We need to go!" Both boys took off running. I was happy to join them.

What followed was the first of many visits I made to the school over the next few years. Once the boys reached the school, they disappeared inside. I sat at the entryway for a while. One thing was clear to me from the beginning about Barrymore High School. This school was dog-friendly, for sure. I knew because there was a dog picture on the flag near the front door. I was delighted to learn later that the school mascot was an Alaskan husky.

Several young people passed by me as they entered the school. Some greeted me with friendly words and gestures, which I appreciated. I was still wary, but these young people meant no harm. I was sure of that. I can tell you what some of them said.

"Hey, doggy, what's your name?" Or "Hey mutt, where's your bookbag?" One joker said, "Hey, Lassie, we're dissecting animals in Biology today. Would you like to volunteer?"

One even said, "Dog. What stink hole did you crawl out from?"

This sudden attention from so many humans made me a little skittish, so I went back to Babe's house, where I knew Babe would return. The sun was shining, and the snow was beginning to melt. I felt good! When I climbed the steps to the front porch, I noticed Mom looking out the window at me. She was smiling. That made me feel doubly good. Over time, I grew to love Mom. She was special. Mom always looked and smelled good, especially when baking bread and pies, which she did a lot. She was a petite woman and was well-loved and respected by her family, especially Dad. Mom wore dresses, usually with an apron on top because of her fabulous cooking.

A few hours later, Babe appeared from around the corner barn and ran up the path to the front porch. I met him as he bounded up the steps and onto the porch. We sat together for a long time, loving each other and relishing our newfound companionship. Finally, he announced, "Well, it's time for you to get a bath, boy."

I didn't know what he was talking about, but I soon found out. He went into the garage and brought out a long rubber hose. Then he headed around to the backside of the house, dragging the hose. About that time, Mom came out on the porch.

"What are you going to do, son?"

"I'm going to give him a bath."

"Good, he needs it. But you're going to have to change your clothes first."

Babe frowned, then said, "Guess what, Mom?"

"What?"

"I've decided on a name for him."

"Oh? What is it, Stinky?"

"Ah, come on, Mom, get serious. I'm naming him Speed."

"Why, that's a great name, Babe. Speed, I like it. Now, go change your clothes, okay?"

Babe patted me and said, "Wait here, Speed. I'll be right back." He disappeared into the house. No problem, I was happy to wait. I wouldn't have been so happy if I had known what he had in mind for me.

In a few minutes, Babe was back. "Speed. Here. Speed, come here!" He was looking at me and pounding himself on his knee, using that word repeatedly. Finally, I realized "Speed" must be me. That was much better than "Boy."

I happily trotted to Babe but immediately found myself standing under a spray of cold water and covered with soap suds from the back of my ears to the end of my tail. Babe worked me over with strong hands going up, down, and around every part of me. Babe expected me to stand still and suffer through all this mistreatment, but I was cold and shivering like crazy. I tried to break away, but Babe raised his voice at me for the first time.

"No, you don't, young man. You are not going anywhere!" He grabbed a handful of my fur and pulled me in close. "Stay here!" I knew he meant business with that voice, so I did what he said. By now, Babe's teeth were chattering. He was as cold and as wet as I was. For me, this was the first of many lessons in obedience training.

After a thorough scrubbing, Babe finished the job by removing all the soap with a soft water spray. Then he wrapped me up in a huge towel and dried me all over. I liked that part. Babe was gentle, and I knew right then that I loved him with all my heart and would do anything for him. Babe had become essential in my life in just a few days. He was my master, and no one else mattered.

The following days were much the same. The boys and I would head out every morning to deliver the *Portland Oregonian*, come home, eat breakfast, and walk the block and a half to school. Babe always got back home first. Den was old enough to play high school football, so he had to stay late for practice. That was fine with me. I had Babe to myself, and we would roughhouse together in the backyard for hours.

It wasn't all play. In those days, we had obedience training sessions, during which Babe taught me specific commands such as "come," "sit," "stay," "quiet," "here," and "lay down." His command to come off those positions was always "Okay."

Babe was patient and always rewarded me with a treat each time I got it right. This routine never became tiresome to me. I enjoyed his attention and the goodies that came with success. Babe always had encouraging words for me as well. He would say, "Good boy, Speed." Then he would grab me around the neck and wrestle me down, and we would roll around on the ground together and love one another. These times were the happiest moments of my life. And I believe they were for Babe too.

We played ball a lot, as well. I never got tired of that. He would throw the ball, and I would run after it, time after time. And let me tell you, Babe had a good arm. He could throw the ball a long way, but he also made short tosses so I wouldn't have to run so much. I never got so tired that I did not want to chase after the ball every time he threw it. Dad would drive in from work towards the end of the day, look at Babe and me, smile, and then go inside the house. He seemed happy I had become part of his family.

It's time to introduce another family member: a bob-tailed cat named Fergie. Fergie was as unfriendly as she was unpretty. She was a stray who had shown up two or three years before I arrived. I can explain Fergie's and my relationship in one word: toleration. We tolerated one another. I didn't even know she existed until one day when she poked her head around the corner of the house and did her "meow" thing, which was really more of a spine-grating and unusual "yowrl." This unpleasant noise woke me from a peaceful front porch nap. I had no idea at the time that Fergie was a member of our family. If I had, I would have saved myself a lot of trouble. But because of my ignorance, I decided this unwelcome visitor needed to go.

As the cautious kitty slinked her way up the steps to the porch, I hunched my body into attack mode, focusing on the target, her neck. Lowering my head and shoulders with my ears laid back, I charged at full speed, expecting her to turn and run for the nearest tree to climb or fence to breach. Instead, this sinister feline humped her back, planted her feet, and stood her ground. She enhanced her defense with a threatening hiss. This sign of fearlessness caused me to pull up short of her nose but, unfortunately, not short of her reach. Before I knew it, she hit me with a vicious left hook, her claws deeply puncturing my tender nose. This blow sparked instant pain and a flow of blood, changing the snow's color beneath our eight feet to a deep shade of red. To say I was shocked would be a classic understatement.

I was embarrassed and wisely sat down to consider my options. My wisest choice would be to seek a peace treaty. My tongue was so busy licking up the blood spurting from my nose that I felt silly and had no desire to consider a second option. I sat there licking my nose and staring at a vicious animal. Fergie returned my gaze with indifference, then turned away from me and began to clean her lethal weapon with her tongue.

So that is how Fergie and I spent our first few minutes getting acquainted. I was licking and looking, contemplating my next move. She ignored me and continued to clean her paw. Finally, she looked at me and winked. She winked! How humiliating was that? Meeting Fergie was not something I remember with pleasure. Fortunately, we lived under a truce of mutual toleration after that and had no further conflicts.

CHAPTER 5

A LOOK BACK

I know very little about my family. I had brothers and sisters, but I had no idea what had happened to them. I know this much: one day, a human showed up and took me away from my mom and siblings. He locked me in a small tool shed when I was young and kept me there. It was solitary confinement, and I was not too fond of it. As I grew, he confined me to his backyard and tied me to a post on a long rope. He would sometimes jerk me around and beat me, usually when drunk. Whenever I smelt alcohol on him, I knew I was in for a beating. His addiction caused him to act that way. I hated him then, but now I understand the problem. He became addicted to alcohol and needed help but had none.

Everything changed the day another man showed up. I was about eight months old at the time. I remember the occasion well. It was late one summer afternoon. The two men spent some time in the backyard sitting on the tailgate of the new man's pick-up truck. They talked for a long while as they drank their liquor.

They also ate sandwiches that smelled delicious. I was hungry, but neither man offered to share with me. Occasionally, feeling anxious and forgotten, I sat and let out a whine or short bark, hoping for a bite of food. They ignored me, so I lay down again at the end of my rope, watching them continue to talk and wishing I could escape. I seriously disliked both men. They would laugh, look at me, raise their bottle, drink, and gobble more food.

"So, what's his name?" the visitor asked.

"Einstein."

"Einstein? Why do you call him that? Is he smart or something?"

My owner tipped up the bottle, took a measured sip, swished it in his mouth, and gulped it down. Then he looked back at me. "Smartest dog you'll ever meet. When Einstein looks at you, he cocks his head and locks on to your eyes. That shows he is listening and trying to understand what you're saying."

"Hmm…yeah, now that you mention it, I did notice that."

"Besides that, his breed is the most intelligent in all dogdom."

"Really? What is he anyway? It looks like he's got some collie blood in him."

"Hey, you're a smart man yourself. Yeah, he's a collie, but not the long-haired pointy-nosed collie you see in dog shows. I call those 'sissy collies.' No sir. This dog is a different kind of collie. It makes him special. You don't often see this kind of collie. Not in this country anyway."

"Oh yeah? What kind of collie is he?"

"This dog is a Scotch collie!"

"Scotch collie? Never heard of that one."

"Yep, that's what I'm saying. This breed of dog is unknown in these parts. Einstein is a <u>gen-u-ine</u> Scotch collie. You know, man, Scotch!" At that point, my owner held up the bottle and laughed. "Scotch! <u>*GEN-U-INE*</u> Scotch! Just like what you're drinking." After another swallow, he handed the bottle to the visitor and wiped his mouth on his shirt sleeve.

"Yep, this the smartest dog I ever owned. You're gettin' a bargain with my man Einstein here. I did some studying on Scotch collies and learned another name for them—farm collie. They make good farm dogs, herding sheep and cows. You know, animals such as that. Very smart. Part of the herding breed. Einstein will make you a crackerjack of a dog."

The visitor took a final swig, handed the bottle back to my owner, and hopped down from the back of the truck. "It's getting dark," he said. "I gotta long way to drive tonight." He looked at me and stumbled over to where I was sitting.

"Come on, Eckstine, or whatever your fool name is." He untied my leash, a worn-out rope, picked me up, and threw me into the back of his truck.

Be careful, man. That hurt!

With clumsy hands, he fumbled around, searching deep into both pants pockets, finally coming up with several dollars and handing them over to my former owner.

"Twenty bucks, right?"

"Huh! Not hardly. This dog is a bargain at fifty, and I'm lettin' you have him for thirty-five. Wise up, man!"

The visitor paused, then said, "Listen here, I ain't never paid cash money for a dog before, that's for sure, let alone thirty-five dollars. This mutt better be as smart as you said he is, or I'm bringing him back and getting a refund, that's for sure! You got that? I mean it now." He reached into his pocket, pulled out a few more bills, and slapped them into the outstretched hand of my recent owner.

"You've never had a dog as smart as Einstein before. That's for sure!"

"Yeah. Well, I will tell you one thing. This mutt will get a new name. I ain't calling him no Einstein, that's for sure. Maybe I'll call him Buck. He cost me a pretty buck, that's for sure."

"You can call him whatever you like, that's for sure!"

I could tell my new owner was mad. Maybe he didn't appreciate being mocked. That didn't help my case any, that's for sure. He jerked open the door to his truck, jumped inside, and we sped away, spewing gravel everywhere. He swerved at the last minute to miss a chunk of firewood that had fallen from a rick stacked alongside a narrow road leading to a paved street. Then he over-corrected, and we swung out into an empty lot, bouncing in and out of a deep hole before returning to the gravel road. His erratic driving caused me to fly from one side of the truck bed to the other, smashing my shoulder and rib cage against the side of the bed. I was not impressed with my new owner's driving, but it didn't matter because I wasn't planning to be with him long anyway. I sensed freedom lurking in the shadows and would grab it at my first opportunity.

Even to a sober driver, the trip over Tollgate is precarious at night. There are curves and switchbacks in a terrain of steep inclines followed by sharp downgrades, which kept me on my feet and leaning against the side of the truck that night. These circumstances didn't bother me. I saw them as opportunities to make my getaway. I noticed the driver had to slow down to a crawl each time the old truck labored to climb a steep grade, and there were plenty of those. I waited for the right moment, and when it came, I went over the side.

I'm not sure my new owner noticed my departure, because he didn't stop. He hit the decline and kept on truckin' down that mountain road. And I kept on truckin' too. I had my first taste of freedom, and I was excited and proud. I had no idea where I was or where I was going. No worries. The road was paved and gradually descending, making for easy travel. Wherever it led would be okay because I was free. No human beings were in my life, and that was what I wanted.

The mountain air was refreshing, and there was very little traffic on Tollgate that night. Occasionally I had to move to the edge of the road to get out of harm's way. I kept my head up as I strutted along, breathing in fresh gulps of mountain air. I felt empowered by my newfound freedom. The night was beautiful, with a full moon lighting the sky above and the highway ahead. I was super excited.

After several hours of moving steadily, I heard the gurgling water of a small creek off to my right. I took a break to wander over and refresh myself with several sweet, clear mountain water drinks. A few small deer were enjoying the water. They stared at me for a few seconds, probably wondering who and what they were looking at, before returning to the creek.

At that moment, a large barn owl flew over us and landed in a massive fir tree that rose high into the night sky. As he landed, he locked his sharp claws onto a limb of the enormous tree. He shook his magnificent body, then gazed down at me and blinked. I returned his gaze. His eyes were so large it took a long time for him to open and close them, so there was a lot more going on behind those eyes than just a blink. I was impressed with this bird's prominent and commanding appearance and how well he had nailed such a perfect pinpoint landing.

Wow! I need to meet this creature! He looks so attractive. Maybe he will be willing to share some of his secrets with me.

I trotted over, put my front feet on the tree's trunk, and looked up at the wise old owl. Our eyes locked up for several seconds, ending in a short "hoot" from my new friend on the tree limb. I looked up at him and gave him a friendly bark.

"Hello, Mister. I'm a dog. A Scotch collie. I'm supposed to be smart. At least that's what I hear."

"Well, hello to you Mr. Dog. I'm an owl. I'm supposed to be wise among the animals. I'm pleased to meet you. Are you from around these parts?"

"No. I just got here. I jumped off the back of a truck."

"Yes, I know. I saw you when you jumped. Then I decided to follow you."

"Really? How come you did that?"

"I like adventuresome animals. But I think you need some wisdom to go along with your smarts. So, I'm going to keep my eye on you if that's okay."

"That would be fine with me. May I call you Hootie?"

"That would be fine."

He hooted again, never taking his eyes off me. I think he would have liked it if I had stayed and spent some time with him, but it was not to be, not that night anyway. After a few more vocal exchanges between us, it soon became apparent that Hootie had decided to settle in for the night. That was okay for him, but I had to keep moving. I was hungry and tired, and I needed to find something to eat and a place to sleep.

"Goodbye, Hootie," I barked. "I hope we meet again someday."

"Oh, we will. As I said, I'll be keeping my eyes on you."

After a few more miles of downhill time, the highway began to level out, and I began to see the twinkling lights of a town. I had arrived on the outskirts of Barrymore, Oregon, where I lived the rest of my earthly life. As I said earlier, no one ever cared about me until I met Babe and his family. But that's okay, because in Babe, I had a master I could love and serve forever.

I live in heaven now. From this vantage point, even though I'm just a lowly dog, I am a creature designed, created, and loved by God. On Earth, Babe was my master. Whether you realize it or not, you also have a Master. He loves you very much, so much that He died for you. On Earth, my only desire was to please my master. I would have died for him if necessary. Your greatest desire should be to love and serve your Master. Why? Because He is the one who suffered and died on the cross so you could live here in heaven one day.

CHAPTER 6
PROMOTION

Life with my master was fantastic. I could not imagine it could ever be better. Wrong! I was surprised when Babe came out of the house one cold December morning and knelt beside me on the porch. He had a king-sized grin on his face.

"Good morning, Speed. I have some good news for you." He cupped my head in his hands and continued. "Mom decided it was too cold for you to sleep outside, so she told me you could move inside. Do you hear that? You don't have to sleep out here on the porch anymore. No sir! You're uptown now, buddy. You're moving inside. I'll fix you a bed in the furnace room—a permanent bedroom for you, starting tonight. Your bedroom will be right next to Den's and my bedroom. How does that sound?"

Babe's excitement was contagious. I wagged and wiggled in anticipation of what was coming. Babe stood up and walked to the front door. "Come on," he said. "I'll show you around." I felt uneasy entering the house and stayed close to Babe. He led me through the living room, dining room, and kitchen. Then we went down some steps into a large laundry room. We walked past the boys' bedroom on the right and into the furnace room on the left.

"This is it," he said. "These are your new digs. No more sleeping out on the porch. You'll be nice and warm and next to Den and me." Again, he dropped to one knee and gave me a tight hug. "This is a big deal, Speed. You now have a room of your own. No more cold nights. No more street noises to keep you awake. Sleep in as long as you like. Congratulations."

Guess what? Even though Mom originally intended that my house privileges be limited to the furnace room, that arrangement lasted just a few weeks. In a short time, I had full house privileges. I ate my meals in the laundry room, but that was it.

After that, I was in every room Babe was in. Even Dad got used to me in the house, and I loved that. Occasionally, I put my nose against his leg while he was sitting in his chair. Dad seemed okay with that, except when he was asleep, of course. I had no problem knowing when he was sleeping because he snored like crazy whenever he kicked back to take a nap. Dad had a snout almost as long as mine, which probably caused him to snore. Dad tried his best to hide his feelings about me, but he often reached down to give me friendly pats when no one was looking.

"Hey buddy, how're you doing?" he would whisper. "You're a good dog." Then he would lay his newspaper down and scratch behind my ears. I loved Dad. However, he sometimes had a quick temper with Mom and the boys. I was not too fond of that. He sometimes apologized for those outbursts but never seemed to get them under complete control.

As you might have guessed, it wasn't long before I slept with Babe. I remember the first time it happened. Babe was on his top bunk with his legs dangling over the side of the bed. I was lying on the floor.

"Speed, here," Babe called.

I looked up and wagged my tail, unsure of what he wanted me to do.

"Speed. Here," he repeated.

I stood and walked over to the ladder. Babe patted his knee and said, "Come here, boy."

I put one front paw on the bottom step, followed by the second, and started climbing. I had never been on a ladder before, but I negotiated it well, and within seconds, I was on the top bunk. No problem. I graduated from sleeping on the furnace room floor to sleeping on an excellent mattress on the top bunk. It took me a while to get the hang of climbing down the ladder. I would step down the top three steps and then jump. The floor was slick, so I learned to put on the brakes when I landed to keep from sliding across the room and out the bedroom door. That took some practice to perfect.

There was plenty of room for us both in the bed. There was a porthole window near the head of the bed that Babe cranked open on cool summer nights, and we would both lie there, gazing at the moon and the stars glimmering on the horizon. My life was complete.

A subtle change had taken place in me. The hate I used to carry was gone, displaced by my love for Babe and his family. Because of my new family, I could no longer hate anyone. Love for my master had overcome all the hate I once had.

When summer came that year, Babe and I went everywhere together. He and his neighbor Dale spent a lot of time together. They loved to fish, so on many occasions, they would take off on their bikes and head to Indian Creek, a spot known for excellent trout fishing. Getting to the place the boys liked to fish took a ten-mile bike ride through farm country.

We would start early, and the boys would have lines in the water by mid-morning. One would make his way upstream and the other downstream. I always had a blast. At first, I splashed around and chased after the many critters who lived there, but after hearing a harsh "Speed, be quiet!" a few times, I learned to stay away from where they were fishing. And I got as excited as they did when one of them would latch onto a large rainbow trout.

After several hours of fishing, the boys would return to their bikes. Their creels were at least half full of fish, and they would spend time talking about the big ones that got away. I remember one rainbow trout Babe caught was too big to get into his creel. Fortunately, he had a large metal basket on his bike. He was able to secure the fish for the long ride back home.

The summer months went by quickly that year, and it was soon time for school to start again. Babe had graduated from grade school and given up his paper route, knowing he would have to free up more time for studies and school activities. He turned out for the high school football team.

Babe and Den always came home from school and did their chores, mainly splitting wood and bringing it in for the kitchen stove. After dinner, they had to take turns washing and drying the dishes before we could do anything fun. Mom made sure of that, backed up by Dad, of course. A coal-fired furnace heated the house, so the boys had to fill the coal hopper in the furnace room daily in the winter. Our playtimes were less frequent because of Babe's need to study and run with his buddies, but I was always part of the group. We had fun, and I was the only non-human invited to participate.

CHAPTER 7
KILROY

Our family took in a guest when school was over for the year. Babe's brother Ken and his family were moving from Seattle to Denver, Colorado, so their dog Kilroy came to spend the summer with us. Kilroy was a spaniel mix, or more descriptively, a mix-up. He was an obnoxious fellow. I realized why people referred to us as dumb animals when I met him. I hate to sound mean, but at the time, I saw this city slicker as a dumb animal, if there ever was one. And it became my job to watch out for him, educate him, and keep him from getting into trouble—a large order.

"Keep your eye on him," Babe whispered in my ear. "I promised my brother we would take good care of him. We can take him fishing with us. We'll show him what real country living is like."

I didn't understand what was happening then, but I soon realized I now had a competitor for Babe's attention. And I knew Babe expected me to be gracious, which wouldn't be easy. The last thing I wanted was an outsider to become part of our life. For starters, I had to share meals with this guy. I realize I had a poor attitude, but that's how I felt. The worst part was having to share my Babe time.

Early on, it became clear that this city dog did not know how to defend himself. I had to bail him out of at least a half-dozen fights the first couple of weeks he was in town. Not only that, but he also barked all the time, especially at birds. We had an abundance of birds around our house. They were friendly little birds: robins, sparrows, and blue jays. He chased all of them away whenever they came around. We had mockingbirds too. These mockingbirds gave Kilroy grief every chance they could. They would dart down to him, almost landing on him. He would bark and play the tough guy trying to scare them away, but they were not the least bit afraid of him. Sometimes, it was amusing to watch. Kilroy never tired of it. Neither did the birds.

Of course, Kilroy was always the little gentleman when humans came around, jutting his speckled muzzle into the air and prancing around, trying to look important. I'll admit Kilroy was a beautiful animal. He was white with black spots or maybe black with white spots. His ears were black, and the fur on them was curly. Babe usually kept us both brushed and looking our best. I didn't hate Kilroy, but I didn't love him either. I tolerated him as best I could.

Toleration worked for a while, but the time finally came when I knew I needed to take Kilroy down a few pegs. I don't mean beating him up or anything. That would not be the right thing to do. Kilroy needed a hefty dose of reality. Life in the country for a dog was more than prancing around chasing harmless birds on a nice carpet of green grass every day or eating a bowl of dog food someone purchased in a grocery store. Kilroy needed to grow up. He needed to experience the challenge of roughing it in situations where bad things could happen, and good things didn't come about without a degree of pain.

I could help him with that. After all, I was a dog who had survived a lot of adversity in my day. He probably wouldn't like it, but the experience would serve him well.

One bright sunny morning, Kilroy and I headed out of town, ready for whatever adventure the day might hold. We traveled west over the foothills toward Tollgate. Tollgate is a rugged forest area, very steep and challenging. We tracked upstream alongside Philips Creek, which runs next to the highway I had traveled to town on months earlier. We stayed off the pavement, though, because there were a lot of large logging trucks going back and forth. I kept the creek between us and the highway, even though it forced us to travel on rough, rocky ground.

The creek was more like a river because it was springtime, and the melted snow was charging down the mountainside, stirring up rapids and causing some flooding. I knew the area well because it was one of the fishing creeks Babe and his neighbor Dale had taken me to the year before. I was excited to retrace our steps—what great memories. Dale, Babe, and I crossed over Philips Creek back and forth, heading upstream as the boys sought out a busy rapid emptying into a quiet pool of fresh water. That's where the fish were, and no one was better at getting them out of the water than my two fishing partners. No one had more fun than I did on these incredible adventures.

Kilroy was having fun as we trotted alongside Philips Creek. So was I. It had been a while since I was in the woods, venturing with my best friend Big and surviving those many months on Hogsback. However, those days were in the past and long gone. Life was so much better for me now, and this trip should be good for Kilroy, which was my intent from the beginning. It would be something he would never have a chance to experience living in a big city. Besides, I didn't figure we'd be gone long. We could cover a lot of ground and possibly be home before dark.

Kilroy chased anything that moved: chipmunks, squirrels, opossums, and the birds that flew close. He had a stare-down with a slithering garter snake and almost got tangled up with a raccoon. Fortunately for Kilroy, the raccoon escaped. Kilroy's hunting instincts drove him to chase whatever came within range of his tenacious nose. Most larger animals, such as deer and the occasional antelope, kept their distance but seemed okay with us invading their territory. They would stare intently at us for a time and then go back to whatever they were doing before we came into view.

Despite the many distractions, we made good progress up the foothills toward the Blue Mountain range. Initially, we moved quickly but then got bogged down in thickets of heavy underbrush and scrub pine trees. The steepening incline slowed our progress to a near snail's pace, and I wondered if we should turn back. Then, as if by God's design, we popped onto a beautiful, expansive open meadow teeming with life. We saw thousands of bright red and yellow flowers, primarily Olympic onion and common silverweed, sprinkled with dandelions and bright yellow buttercups. Bordering the meadow on all sides was a mix of ferns and pussy willows with an occasional Ponderosa pine tree stretching high into the sky.

Dogs are colorblind in the world, but I have perfect sight now that I live in heaven. I can call up a vision of the beauty of that place and see the colors there. Heaven is an incredible place to live. There is nothing like it anywhere. You can see whatever you want to see and see it perfectly. Why would any creature turn away from the God who created it and makes it available just for the asking?

What a peaceful and glorious place we discovered that morning. Two or three small streams ran through it, downhill to Philips Creek. I told myself there were probably lots of fish in those streams, and I might be able to lead Babe and Dale there that summer. The streams were generously bordered by pussy willows and cattails, some as tall as six feet or more. There were scatterings of molehills and groundhog burrows. We had fun chasing these critters into their homes, followed by furious digging on our parts, but to no avail.

We roamed through the entire area. A small pond looked interesting at the meadow's far end, especially to Kilroy. He made a mad dash for the pond because he saw some furry animals working extremely hard on a building project at the head of the stream that fed the pond. As soon as Kilroy arrived, several creatures disappeared below the waterline with startling slaps of their gigantic flat tails. Kilroy, about twenty paces ahead of me, was not deterred. He plunged into the pond and began to swim around, looking at his first victim, a massive beaver in a colony of beavers who had been busy adding structure to their dam before Kilroy arrived.

As for me, I stopped at the water's edge for two reasons. I was not as impulsive as Kilroy, but the more significant reason was that one giant beaver held his ground and positioned himself between me and the pond. At first, he seemed uninterested in having a showdown with me, as he was gnawing on a large limb and spitting out chips as big as silver dollars. He looked nasty, and when he finally looked at me, he bared his front teeth, four sharp-looking incisors. He also made threatening hissing sounds. He sat well balanced on his sizeable flat tail, daring me to start trouble.

"What you got, mutt?"

With that, I decided against an all-out attack. Seeing his razor-sharp teeth and mean-looking claws and hearing those threatening hissing noises intimidated me. Truthfully, "he scared the daylights out of me" would be a more honest way of describing it. But I knew I had to do something. So, I looked him in the eye and barked,

"You better get out of my way, rodent! I'm a Scotch collie! You ever heard of a Scotch collie before?"

"No, I'm afraid I haven't. Have you ever been in a fight with an irate beaver before?"

I knew I didn't want to pursue that possibility, so I strung a series of barks together, making threatening movements in his direction, but at a safe distance. I knew I could outrun him if nothing else. My barking didn't bother him. Finally, he grew tired of looking at me and turned his back, showing complete disdain for my false bravado. He slipped into the water, not even offering me the respect of a tail slap before disappearing.

Meanwhile, Kilroy grew weary of swimming around the pond and looking for trouble, and he came out of the water. He was exhausted, and so was I. The sun was disappearing behind the western skyline, so we trotted to a bench-like knoll that offered warm sunshine and a soft grass bed. It didn't take us long to fall asleep.

When we woke up the next day, we were hungry. "We need to head home," I said to Kilroy, and I turned back toward the meadow's edge. Kilroy immediately fell in behind me, but before we had gotten very far, he shot out in front of me to check out a bristly animal he'd spotted near the meadow's edge. This strange-looking creature came into view before disappearing down a narrow trail before us. Of course, Kilroy immediately gave chase, and the two animals escaped into thick brush. Expecting trouble, I followed cautiously. It took me several minutes to reach the crime scene.

When I got there, the bristly one was gone, but Kilroy was there, and sadly, he had acquired many of the animal's bristles in his nose and face. He was a mess, especially his nose. My traveling partner was down on the ground, digging with both paws to trying and extract the multitude of quills poking out in every direction from his nose and face. He gave me a pained grimace, whined, and returned to the task at hand.

"Sorry, Buddy," I said. "But we've got a long way to go."

I felt sorry for him, but there was no way I could help him other than get him back home where Babe could take care of him. I continued down the trail. He followed, shaking his head violently, attempting to dislodge the quills. It was a good lesson for both of us, but more painful for Kilroy.

When we finally got to Philips Creek, we stopped and refreshed ourselves, lapping the cool water. At least I did. It was hard for Kilroy to drink much water. He pricked his tongue on the quills whenever he stuck it out to clear the water off. That was not pretty. We rested for a while, which we both needed, but we were both hungry and knew our only food possibilities were at home.

The sun had begun to rise on the eastern horizon when I decided it was time to move out again. I took the lead, heading east alongside the south side of the creek. The shadows were still dark, so we moved carefully through the underbrush.

It was mid-morning when at last we trotted into the yard of our home in Barrymore. Fortunately, it was Saturday, so Babe and Den were not in school. They heard us when we plopped down on the front porch.

"Hey, boys, where have you guys been?" Babe shouted as the boys stepped outside and walked across the porch. Babe dropped to one knee to hug me. Then he looked over at Kilroy.

"Oh my gosh, Den, look at Kilroy!"

"Yeah, it looks like he got tangled up with a porcupine. His face is a mess."

Babe leaned over to get a closer look at Kilroy's face. He carefully cradled him in his arms. "Man, he has quills everywhere. Just look at his nose!"

I can attest that a dog's nose is a delicate organ. Fortunately, blood was not pouring out, but there was a bubble of blood at the base of each quill protruding from Kilroy's nose, and there must have been seven or eight quills in that part alone.

Kilroy looked plaintively into Babe's eyes, clearly pleading for help. "I've got to get those quills out of there," Babe said, looking up at Den.

"I agree, little brother, but I can't help you now. I can't be late for football practice." Den had made the varsity team that year and was the starter at left guard. He said, "You can handle it, Babe," and turned and hustled down the steps.

Babe looked over at me as if asking for some hidden insight. I walked around, put my nose under his arm, and gave it an encouraging boost.

"You're right, Speed. We need to take care of this right now."

Fifteen minutes later, the three of us were in the utility room. Babe had found an old gunnysack, pulled it over and around Kilroy, and tucked the opening under the leather collar Kilroy was wearing. Only Kilroy's head was sticking out of the sack. Babe had the dog on his back, lying on a carpet as he straddled him, yielding a pair of pliers in his right hand. Then, one by one, Babe jerked out the quills from Kilroy's nose and cheeks. It was a painful thing to watch.

Throughout the process, Babe talked to Kilroy, using soothing and encouraging words. "You'll be okay, Kilroy. I know it hurts. We both do, don't we Speed? You're a brave dog, Kilroy. I bet that porcupine was scared to death of you. Hold on, buddy. We're just about done. Good boy, Kilroy. Good boy."

After Babe pulled out the last one, fifteen quills lay scattered around the concrete floor. Fortunately, there had been no quills in or near his eyes. We were all glad when the job was complete, especially Kilroy. He busied his tongue, cleaning and soothing the affected areas.

Mom brought a clean, damp rag for Babe to dab the wounds. After several minutes of tender strokes around Kilroy's neck and ears, Babe pulled the gunnysack from around Kilroy's body and pushed a fresh bowl of water before him so he could get a nice cold drink. When that ordeal was over, we dogs got baths, and Kilroy got to sleep on the boy's bedroom floor, snuggled in a soft blanket. As I laid my head against Babe's body that night, I felt a renewed love and respect for my master. He had been very tender toward Kilroy.

Kilroy's and my shared experience brought us closer together. I felt I had accomplished my mission. Kilroy had picked up a taste of country living and had some fun. Unfortunately, he still had a great deal to learn.

CHAPTER 8

IT TOOK FOREVER

I knew something was up that first week in July as I went from room to room and watched my family pack clothes into suitcases. When the boys finished packing, they lugged their bags outside, where Dad muscled them into the trunk of the family car. I became uneasy and sensed Babe was not comfortable either. *What's going on here? Are we all going somewhere? A trip with four people and two dogs would make for a crowded car.*

I went over to Babe and bumped up against his leg. It was not unusual for me to bump up against my master's leg, but the mood was different, and my bump was more rigorous than usual. He squatted down and gave me a big hug. I loved the hug, but I could feel some tension at the same time.

"It's okay, Speed. Our family is going on a little vacation for a few weeks."

The word "vacation" sounded strange to me, because whenever I had heard it before, it had always been used along with "summer," as in "summer vacation." Those were two words I loved to hear. Hearing it without the word "summer" attached to it was strange, especially with what was happening with the suitcases.

About that time, Dale came walking across our yard. He knelt and started loving on Kilroy and me.

"Hey, boys," he said as he pulled us to him. "You guys are going to belong to me for a while now. You better get used to it. I'm not going to let you get away with anything! Do you hear that? No funny stuff, guys, from either one of you!" I glanced at Kilroy. He just sat there with his tongue hanging out, clueless as usual.

Both boys stood up to help Dad, who had brought two more suitcases to the car. Together, they hoisted them into the car's trunk. Then Dad closed the trunk lid, turned to his family, and with a huge, satisfied smile, asked, "Are you all ready for this adventure to begin?"

At that point, my instincts directed me to move between Babe and the car. Babe dropped down to his knees again and gave me a long hug.

He spoke softly into my ear and said, "I'll be back, Speed. Don't worry. Dale will be taking care of you and

Kilroy. You listen to him and do what he tells you." He pulled me in close. "Keep your eye on Kilroy. You know how he can get into trouble in a hurry. Stay cool. I'll be back before you know it, and when I get back, we'll pick it up where we left off, okay, buddy? So be ready. Nothing bad will happen, I promise. I love you, Speed. You're my best friend, and I'll miss you, buddy."

I knew he was going to leave me even though he didn't want to. *Where is my master going? How long will he be gone? He told me he would be back soon, but how soon? And back from where?* He wanted me to stay on the alert and be good. He didn't have to tell me that. I probably wasn't always good, but I was always "on the alert" for my family.

He reached Kilroy, who had crept up to us and propped his head on Babe's leg. He said to both of us, "Dale will be looking after you guys until I get back. Listen to him and do what he tells you, okay? He pulled us both together. "You guys are in charge. Guard the house, and don't let strangers move in and take over. Okay? You got that?" He gave us both simultaneous hugs and rose to his feet. "I love you guys. Be good and listen to Dale."

I grew anxious when I saw Dad get into the car, followed by the rest of the family—the human side, anyway. Dad started the car and slowly backed down the driveway. Babe rolled down his back window. His head came out, then his arm.

"Hey, Speed. Take care of things while I'm gone. Okay? I'll be back, I promise." He kept looking at me as the car stopped at the end of the driveway and then proceeded down the street. He looked sad. I started to run after the car, but Dale caught hold of my collar and held me back.

"Hold on, Speed," he said. "He'll be back. Relax."

When the car disappeared, I could hardly believe what was happening. The whole family was going away somewhere without me. I whined loudly, twisted my neck, and tried to pull away from Dale.

There must be some mistake! How could they do this to me? Does Dale own me now? No, he does not. I belong to Babe!

Kilroy got all nervous and began to run around the yard, jumping and yelping. He didn't know what he was doing. He became so hyper that he tried to get me into a wrestling match by attacking me and clamping down on my front right leg. I was in no mood for Kilroy's antics and let him know it by a nasty snarl and grabbing a mouthful of his floppy left ear. That scared the daylights out of him. He released a weak yelp and disappeared up the steps and onto the porch. I realized this was not nice, but I wasn't in a loving mood.

That night, Dale fed us and let us into the back of the house. Kilroy settled in his bed right away, but I found myself wandering through the house, going from room to room, hoping to discover that some family member had returned suddenly. Of course, I found no one. All the rooms were empty and lonely looking. It seemed so odd not having my family home where they belonged. Finally, I returned to the boys' bedroom and climbed the ladder to Babe's and my bed. It took me a long time to go to sleep. I kept listening for the car to return, but it didn't.

The next several days and nights were the longest of my life. *Where is Babe? How could he do this to me? Will my family ever come home again? Does he miss me?*

Dale cared for us, but it was not the same without Babe. Dale came over each morning and let us out of the house. He usually brought us some treats or a bone to chew on. Dale also made sure Fergie's food dish was never empty.

"There you go, boys," he would say as he placed whatever he had for us to eat into our respective doggy dishes. Then he would return to his house, and we were on our own for the rest of the day. We didn't wander far from home, however. I spent most of my time sitting or lying on the wide ledge of the porch wall, where I could see the road on which Babe left. Babe had promised he would return to me and told me that I should wait, so that's what I did. I needed to be there when my master returned. But it was difficult, and the days seemed endless.

Kilroy was not concerned about any of this. If he had a large bone to gnaw on, he was happy. Dale kept him supplied with plenty of those. Chewing on things never appealed to me. I would watch Kilroy gnaw on a bone for hours with little or no reward. Not my idea of fun.

We slept a lot during the day, usually on the front porch. Occasionally, another dog or a stray cat wandered into the yard. Things like that used to excite me, but now I ignored them. They didn't bother me, but they did bother Kilroy. He would growl, bark like the tough guy he wasn't, bound down the steps, and jump on the dog as if King Kilroy had complete authority over our property. It was humorous, so I decided not to get involved in his battles. If he took a whipping, that was his problem.

During this time, Kilroy met Fergie for the first time. Fergie continued to come and go, but she mostly stayed out of sight, probably due to Kilroy's presence. She would hang out near the wood rick or in the woodshed.

Whenever Kilroy looked her way, Fergie disappeared. Therefore, they never met formally until one memorable afternoon. Kilroy and I were dozing in our usual places on the front porch. The day was uneventful until suddenly Kilroy began to growl, an extended low growl, which was unusual. Kilroy didn't usually growl. He barked. I lifted my head and saw Fergie and Kilroy engaged in an ugly stare-down.

Oh, oh, this is not going to be pretty.

With his eyes on the cat, Kilroy began to inch down the steps toward Fergie. Fergie's back humped up as she waited. Her eyes locked on Kilroy's once gorgeous black nose. Memories of my first meeting with this sultry vixen and her deadly left hook rocketed through my mind. I barked a short warning.

"Kilroy! Stay back!"

Kilroy didn't listen. He continued to advance on his prey, his nose now only inches away from Fergie's lethal left paw.

I barked again. "Kilroy. Watch out!"

Kilroy paid no attention.

"Kilroy, for heaven's sake, back up, you dunderhead."

Unfortunately, Kilroy ignored me a third time. Spaniels are stubborn. He growled at Fergie, which was a fatal mistake. Fergie's punch was delivered with awesome power. Her claws sunk deeply into Kilroy's nose as she let out an earsplitting "Yowrl!"

Why doesn't this cat just say "meow," like other cats do?

Kilroy's nose immediately began spewing blood all over the front steps. Kilroy shrieked in agony as he shot me a look of "WHAT THE HEY?!" Then he ran to my side, dripping blood all along the porch floor. I gave him a sympathetic look, but there was nothing I could do. I had tried to warn him, but he wouldn't listen.

Meanwhile, Fergie yawned, stretched, and rubbed her back against the side of the porch. After a few minutes she gave us both a look of superiority and disappeared.

* * *

As I thought back on this incident in later years, I could see how my feelings toward Kilroy had softened over the summer we had together. Our getaway adventure up Tollgate plus our dependence on one another since Babe's disappearance brought us closer together. And I appreciated his company as we waited for Babe's return. I decided he was not a bad guy—just not very wise. Yes,

I should have treated him better when he first came to us. I know that is what Babe wanted me to do. As I said, you look at things differently once you gain a heavenly perspective.

Everything about heaven is different than on Earth. There's no ill will here. No hatred. Just love. It's impossible to sin here. Of course, sin was never the same problem for our kind when we lived on Earth as it was for humans. In our earthly lives, we never lied or cheated. Therefore, unlike you, we needed no one to pay for our ticket into heaven. We are here because it is our Creator's will that we are here.

Now would be a good time to clarify a few things. A dog in heaven? Certainly! God loves His creation, including all animals. The Bible says that one day, the wolf will dwell with the lamb, and the leopard will lie down with the young goat, the calf, the lion, and the fatling together. And a little boy will lead them.

When God created us, He intended us to live together in a perfect place called Eden, which we did. But then God had to close Eden down because of people's sins. No animal sin was involved. Adam and Eve got kicked out because they disobeyed God.

One day, all creation will be set free from the corruption of sin and into freedom and glory as children of God. This includes all life, not just humans. A book humans call The Gospel of Luke says, "All flesh will see the salvation of God." "All flesh" includes animals, of course. Here are two important things I want you to know, dear reader:

1. Your pet has a home in heaven if you want, and of course, if you are heaven-bound yourself.

2. In heaven, animals can talk. They could speak in Eden, so why would they not be able to talk in heaven? In Eden, a serpent carried on a conversation with Eve. God made a donkey talk as well. It's in your Bible.

I want my master Babe to come up here someday. Babe prayed that I would be with him in heaven, so I'm here now because of his payers. If your future home is heaven, your pet can be with you. Just ask God, who can do anything. Nothing is impossible with Him. His Son is Jesus. And Jesus gives life forever.

CHAPTER 9

THAT SOW WAS HOT

It was four weeks to the day when I heard the familiar sound of the family automobile chugging up Alder Street toward our house. Kilroy and I had spent most of the day napping on the porch. It was late afternoon on a warm day in July. My ears popped up first, and my tail began to pound the porch floor uncontrollably. What was this? Could it be? Then, in unbridled excitement, I jumped up on the porch ledge, where I could see my family coming toward me. It was true!

At last, they were home. As the car pulled onto the driveway, I jumped off the porch ledge and hit the ground running. The first person out of the vehicle was Babe, who jumped out, grinning ear to ear.

"Hey buddy, how are you?" We ran toward one another. From five feet apart, I leaped into his open arms. Babe caught me in mid-air, and we both fell to the ground and rolled around, hugging and kissing each other. He kept asking, "Did you miss me, boy? Did you miss me?"

Did I miss him? Really? He asked me if I had missed him. I missed him enough to swear I would never let him out of sight again. Ever!

My tail was wagging so vigorously that I could not control it. Every part of me was in motion, from my back to my ears. I could not tell if my tail was wagging my booty or my booty was wagging my tail. I had never been happier than I was at that moment. Babe was as excited as I had ever seen him. I knew right then that Babe loved me with all his heart.

I was all over him. No one would have been able to get in between us, although Kilroy tried his best to get in on the action by barking and crazily jumping around in circles. We finally rose to our feet, continuing our exuberant dance together. He held me tight. Our love energy long held in reserve was explosive.

By that time, everyone else was out of the car. They all seemed happy to see us, even Dad, who gave Kilroy and me several love pats as he went to the back of the car and opened the trunk. Finally, we were one big happy family again. This was a day of celebration, a day I will never forget.

"Welcome home," a grinning Dale said to Babe as he walked across our yard from his house.

"Yeah, finally!" Babe replied as the two friends gave one another a quick handshake.

Babe reached into the car trunk and handed Dale a suitcase. "Here you go Dale, make yourself useful." In short order, the car was empty. Soon, the bags and adults, including Den, had disappeared into the house. Left outside were two dogs and two boys. All those nights which seemed so endless were finally behind us. I was so happy. All my family was home again.

"I don't know about you, but I'm ready to go fishing," Babe said. He sat down on the grass and pulled me next to him.

"Sounds good," Dale replied. "How about Tuesday?"

"Works for me," Babe said. Then he cradled my face in his hands and gently rocked my head back and forth. "Are you ready to go fishing, Speed?"

Fishing? Yeah, I knew what that word meant. I jumped up and looked at Babe, barking once, an obvious yes to Babe's question. My bark stirred Kilroy into a barking frenzy. He didn't know what was happening but knew it was something, and he had to join in. Things were looking up. Life would be exciting again.

We were always up early on Sunday mornings because our family's job was to set up the altar and the chairs for the morning service. The church was nearby, so Babe and I walked while the rest of the family drove. Kilroy tagged along. We waited for the service to end so we could walk home with Babe. It was fun. People often gave us a pat or two as they went by. On the way home, Babe would stop occasionally and throw sticks for us to chase.

Sometimes after church, we walked five or six blocks to town to see if our friends were out. Because it was Sunday, most times, they were not. Saturdays were different. On Saturdays, people come to town to shop and visit. Saturday nights were important, especially to the young folks. That is when they did their girlfriend and boyfriend stuff. Babe had no interest in that sort of thing, early on, anyway.

But Sundays were church days, and people took church seriously in Barrymore.

* * *

Around this time, I began noticing certain changes in Babe. His voice was lower in tone. He had also grown taller and more muscular. I think playing football had much to do with that. I occasionally hung out at football practice and watched his team go through their workouts. They were hard-hitting, but Babe always seemed able to hold his own. I didn't particularly like seeing him get banged around, but I sensed it was all okay. Babe was growing up and changing. Several mornings I saw him standing in front of a mirror, shaving some whiskers off his face.

I had no problems with any of the growing-up stuff. That was normal for a human and for an animal too. However, a new reality smacked me between the eyes one morning after church when I saw Babe walking hand in hand with a girl. And he was acting silly.

What is this about?

Babe giggled and swung their two arms up and down as they descended the steps.

"May I escort Mademoiselle to her chariot?" he asked, sweeping his free hand in a circular motion.

The girl giggled, blushed, and looked around, probably hoping no one was watching.

I was more confused by the scene than concerned. It was Babe, after all. He could do anything he wanted as far as I was concerned. I bounced forward to greet him. With a big grin, he pointed to me and said, "This is Speed."

"Hi, Speed," the girl giggled again. She reached out a hand to me, but I didn't respond for some reason, probably the giggling.

Who is this girl?

Whoever she was, she turned me off. I backed away.

"Speed, here!" Babe called me. "What is wrong with you? Come and meet my friend Joan." As I thought about it, Joan was silly and giggly, but other than that, there was no reason for me to behave as I did. The point is, I couldn't see any sense in their friendship. She didn't look like she could catch a fish or a flyball or throw a stick ten feet. But she seemed to like Babe, and he seemed to like her, which was important. Anyway, I soon realized it didn't matter what I thought.

But why is he holding her hand? Where does she fit into our relationship? Nowhere, I hope.

I edged over to where they were standing. Of course, Kilroy had to come over and horn in on the action as well.

"And this is Kilroy," Babe said.

Joan bent down and gave us both friendly but timid pats on the head. "Hello, boys. I am glad to meet you two." Instinctively, we were wagging our tails and acting friendly, but I was not as warm as Kilroy. He bounced around as if he was the attraction of the moment. Finally, Babe had to give him a stern, "Settle down, Kilroy."

Then, of all things, Babe turned away and started talking with Joan, ignoring Kilroy and me. I couldn't believe it. Were we not as important as this silly girl? Babe had never acted this way before. I was confused. Mom and Dad came down the steps, and that was it. Dad announced it was time to go. Babe looked at Joan, smiled, and said, "See you. I'll call you this afternoon, okay?"

As Babe, Kilroy, and I walked home from church, I wondered if I might have to share Babe's affections with this new friend in the days ahead. My fears proved to be on target. Every Sunday, they talked together while their parents visited after church. Then her family would get into their car and drive away. Babe always seemed a little sad on those mornings after church. I didn't understand what was going on. He moped around the house or sat on his bunk for long periods, staring at the wall. Frankly, I found myself hoping her family would not show up for church every Sunday. It made me sad when Babe was sad and mopey, and it always happened after he spent time with this girl.

***

The following Tuesday morning was beautiful. It had rained the evening before, so the air was fresh with a cool breeze whispering through the tall evergreen trees of eastern Oregon. There were many scents in the morning air that day, most of which only Kilroy and I could appreciate. That is an ability animals have that is far superior to humans. Humans have some six million olfactory receptors. Dogs have up to three hundred million, so we're good at smelling. That is why police officers and soldiers love us. We can find hidden things humans cannot locate. Brave dogs work with brave men and women everywhere in the world. Dogs fill a role no other creature on Earth can fill due to our excellent gift of smell.

As we embarked on our fishing trip that Tuesday morning, the boys on their bicycles with Kilroy and me running alongside, we dogs were excited. Kilroy had no idea where we were going, but he was having fun. I remember the distinct aromas of the morning flowers and trees, the human smells, and the animals in the area. We also smelled the newly sawn, green-cut lumber at a nearby sawmill that morning. We could smell auto exhaust, sweet aromas from the local grocery store, and many more scents which I don't remember. Not important. We were going fishing!

It was about ten miles from town to the McCullough ranch. Indian Creek ran through their property, so we always looked for a convenient place to cut through and get to the creek.

"This looks good, Babe," Dale yelled as he stopped at the tip of a sweeping curve in the gravel road. He leaned his bike against the barbed wire fence.

Babe pulled his bike behind Dale's and leaned it against the fence. He removed his fishing rod from the handlebars of his bicycle. Dale did the same, and with their creels and rods, the boys were ready to cross an empty pasture and head for the creek.

"I'll get it," Babe said as he put his left foot on the bottom strand of wire and pulled up on the upper strand with his right hand, allowing Dale to crawl through the fence, carefully avoiding the sharp barbs on the wire. Dale returned the favor by pulling the strands apart for Babe. Of course, I did not wait for the boys to do their thing. I scooted under the lower strand of wire. Kilroy tried doing the same thing, but he got hung up by the barbed wire. Babe moved over, released him from the wire, and held it up to give him ample space to squeeze in.

"There you go, boy," Babe said to Kilroy. He patted his head and checked his back for injuries. Satisfied there were none, he said, "No harm done. Now, behave yourself, buddy. Okay?"

When we were on the other side of the fence, the boys quick-paced through the pasture. At first, we stayed together until Kilroy suddenly swung off. He charged toward a family of pigs on the far end of the field, abruptly followed by an explosion of a dozen squealing baby pigs scattering in every direction. Kilroy was in hot pursuit.

"Kilroy!" Babe shouted at the top of his lungs. "Kilroy, here! Get back here, you idiot!"

But Kilroy wasn't listening. He was having a blast chasing a dozen squealing little animals, the likes of which he had never seen. It was quite a comedy at first, but it suddenly turned ugly. Mama Pig emerged into view. Mama Pig was gigantic and in a nasty mood, understandably so. She was furious that a strange and unmannered pooch was raising havoc with her babies, so she went after Kilroy, who suddenly acquired respect for large pigs.

Both boys hollered at Kilroy to stop. Mama Pig quickly gave up trying to catch Kilroy and zeroed in on Babe, who had charged forward to try to grab Kilroy. "Get out of here, stupid pig," Babe hollered. He took three or four strides toward the furious sow. Babe realized his mistake when Mama Pig redirected her charge toward him, a much slower target. Babe did an immediate one-eighty, but he had no chance.

I knew Babe could not outrun this massive animal, and he risked being seriously hurt as a result. He was on a dead run toward the fence on the other side of the field. He ran as fast as he could, but he was slipping and sliding, and Mama Pig was faster and more capable of running in the soft mud than Babe. Babe was quickly losing the race and would soon have four hundred pounds of angry sausage on top of him. I knew I had to do something or Babe would be badly hurt by this upset mama intent on protecting her brood. So, I joined the chase. The five of us were making a mad, slippery race toward the fence.

Mama Pig was right on Babe's heels when I jumped on her. Yes, that is right. I jumped right on the middle of her back and bit her neck with all the force I could muster. I clamped down severely enough to make her squeal out in pain. Staying aboard this muddy pig was challenging, but she had a broad back. I put some hurt on her by grabbing a mouthful of her hide. I rode her like a cowboy on a wild Brahma bull for fifteen seconds and then exited from her back when I saw Babe was in the clear. She turned on me, but I evaded her easily.

We dashed to the other side, got through the fence, and escaped to the swift-moving creek. The boys were all excited and out of breath when it was over.

"That was close," Dale gasped. He bent over and placed his hands on his knees.

Babe was hot! He grabbed Kilroy by his collar and gave him a terrific bawling out. I had never seen Babe so angry. "You idiot," he said, jerking him to his side. "Chasing after a bunch of baby pigs? I'm ashamed of you, Kilroy. I am never taking you fishing again! Do you hear me? I'm never taking you fishing again. Ever!" He must not have meant it because we had lots of fishing time left that summer. However, he certainly had Kilroy's attention.

Kilroy put his head down. He looked over at me and then pleadingly up at Babe with his big brown eyes. I'm unsure if Kilroy knew where he had screwed up. I know this; Kilroy quickly forgave Babe for his harsh rebuke by sticking his tongue out and licking his hands. That is what we dogs do. We are quick to dismiss any grievance from our human masters.

The balance of the day was uneventful compared to our run-in with the pig family. The boys caught plenty of fish. Kilroy and I managed to stay out of the way. We had fun digging holes in the soft sand, chasing frogs, water skippers, and everything else that moved. And when it was time to leave the McCullough ranch, we found a separate way out to the road, wisely avoiding pig-land.

Babe called Kilroy over and knelt beside him once we reached our bikes. "I'm sorry, Kilroy, for what I said to you. That was mean of me. You are not an idiot. You're just not wise to country living, that's all. You are a good dog, and I'm glad you're here, boy. Do you hear that? I'm glad you're here. So is Dale. So is Speed. We're all glad you're spending the summer with us. Wait until you share this story with your city friends. They'll love it!" He roughed his neck, hugged him, and climbed on his bike.

"Let's go," he said, and we all took off toward Barrymore. The boys pedaled their bikes as fast as they could. With no time to spare, we pulled up in front of our house just as the six o'clock evening siren at the fire station blew, which was our curfew time.

What a day we had. I can guarantee you it was one that none of us would soon forget.

***

In four short weeks, the fun of summer ended once again. Somehow, I knew Kilroy would be leaving us soon, and it made me sad. I think his time with us was good for us all. He had been a bother at times, but we had fun together, so it was well worth it.

We were sad when his family showed up one late summer evening in August to retrieve their pet. Kilroy had an exciting summer. He had experienced a new way of life, a rare treat for a city dog. In a word, I'm proud of Kilroy, proud to have been his friend. Removed from his element, he did well. I wonder if I would have done well if I had spent a summer in a big city. Fortunately, I had no such opportunity.

It took a while for us to all say our goodbyes. I sensed this was permanent because the humans all had to speak to Kilroy. Dale was especially sad as he came over and knelt by Kilroy. "I'll miss you, buddy," Dale said, giving Kilroy a long and loving hug. "You could come back next summer, you know. We could chase some pigs again. What do you think? Huh? What do you think of that? Those little pigs would be grown up by then. You could make friends with them."

Babe's brother Ken heard the conversation. "Pig chasing? What is that about?"

"You don't want to know, big brother," Babe chimed as he sat down on the grass and joined Dale in the group hug with Kilroy. He smiled. "You don't want to know."

Kilroy didn't know what was happening but loved the attention. Babe grabbed him around the neck and gave him a big hug. Kilroy returned the favor with a wet kiss. "We'll miss you, boy. It won't be the same without you. We love you, buddy."

Finally, it was my turn to say goodbye. I walked over to Kilroy and put my head next to his head. "Goodbye, Kilroy. I'm going to miss you a lot. You are a good friend."

Kilroy stood still as our muzzles caressed together. Then he put his nose to my ear and said, "It's been great. Thanks for everything."

Soon after that, Ken loaded up his family, and they backed their station wagon down the driveway and disappeared down Alder Street. I never saw Kilroy again. It seems strange, but I missed him even long after he was gone. I know Babe did as well.

When I first met Kilroy, my goal was to see him change from being a city dog dependent on human care to a dog with a life of independence and freedom like mine. I had little respect for him and, indeed, no love. I wanted to make him like me, something he could not ever be. God makes us all unique to serve his purposes, even animals. After Kilroy left, I realized the change was in me and not so much in Kilroy. I grew as I watched Babe's tenderness and love for Kilroy play out over the summer and during all the time we spent alone together waiting for Babe's return from vacation. My attitude toward him had evolved from dislike to tolerance and from tolerance to love.

CHAPTER 10
YEARBOOK FIASCO

Barrymore High School classes assembled outside the school each spring for class photographs. Students in each grade came out on the school's front porch at an assigned time, and a professional photographer took their class photo. The picture became part of the high school yearbook. It was a big deal to the kids and essential to the school. The students looked forward to it. Miraculously, this event seemed to always happen on a sunny day. The kids loved it because it was a break from the classroom and they could mingle, socialize, and relax together.

Of course, humans sometimes show little sense, especially teenage humans. Forming an organized assembly in groups of twenty or thirty young men and women takes a long time and a lot of patience. Teachers, photographers, and helpers worked hard to bring order to the event.

Babe was a high school sophomore, and when his class came out, I was an unofficial observer. It was not unusual for me to be at school. I liked being around Babe's friends. They all knew me and greeted me by name with pats on the head and an occasional treat, which I appreciated.

On this day, as I hung out and observed the kids assembling on the school's large front porch, from the crowd, I heard someone calling, "Here, Speed. Here, Speed." It sounded like Babe's voice, but it was muffled and soft. The kids were making a lot of noise, but I was sure it was Babe's voice I heard. I cocked my head and looked for him in the assembly of kids gathering on the porch. Then it came again. "Here, Speed," slightly louder and accompanied by a soft whistle. Some other kids began to call me as well.

At last, I spotted Babe. He looked straight ahead, not at me, but I heard him snap his fingers. I knew he needed me then, so I trotted over and mounted the steps to the Class of '53. I positioned myself at the side of the students and stood tall. I wasn't sure why I was there, but Babe and his friends had invited me, making me feel proud and important. We had to hold our position for a long time, which wasn't easy for the kids or for me. Organizing the class by size, with the tall kids in the back, the short kids in front, and the mid-sized ones in the middle, seemed endless. Of course, there was no designated place for dogs, but that was no problem. I was glad to be in the group, and no one asked me to leave.

Unfortunately, even though I had held my pose rigidly, something distracted me right before the photographer snapped the picture. I looked away from the camera the moment the photographer snapped the picture. It was too bad, but that sort of thing always happens. A kid gets distracted at the last minute or reaches out to punch a friend, and the picture gets taken. Well, that's what happened to me. The kids who knew I was there undoubtedly thought it was unique. I was in the yearbook that year as an official class member.

Sadly, the picture-taking session had an unfortunate after-story. When it was over and the kids returned to their classroom, I noticed Superintendent Mr. Boswell pull Babe aside and sternly speak to him. I wasn't sure what was happening then, but I know now.

Mr. Boswell said to Babe, "That was not funny, Babe."

"Sir?" Babe replied.

"Your dog, Speed. What were you thinking, Babe?"

"Well, sir, I'm sorry. It, uh, just happened."

"No, Babe, it just did not 'just happen.'" Mr. Boswell was in Babe's face. "I understand you called your dog to the porch. Is that right?"

Babe's head went down for a moment. Then he straightened up and looked Mr. Boswell in the eye. "Yes, sir."

"Is our education program just one big joke to you, Babe?"

"No, sir. Not at all, sir."

"Our school is not a place for you or any student to compromise our lofty standards. You do realize that, don't you, Babe?"

Still looking Mr. Boswell in the eye, Babe said, "Yes, sir."

"We are known for our excellence and our professionalism." He paused. They were both still eyeball to eyeball. No one blinked. Mr. Boswell continued. "So now, Babe, here's the problem. We will publish our yearbook, which, as you know, we take considerable pride in, right?"

Babe looked down briefly but didn't comment.

"Now we have a decision to make." His tone was now slightly heated as he paused momentarily. Then he said, "Do you know what that might be, Babe?"

Babe returned his gaze to Mr. Boswell and said weakly, "No, sir!"

"That will be whether to produce our yearbook without your class included." He paused again, then added, "Or possibly, with your class of thirty-one students, two teachers, and one dog."

He paused again.

"Do you understand what I am saying, Babe?"

"Yes, I understand, sir, and I'm sorry."

Mr. Boswell paused once more, then capped the conversation with a crushing, "Don't figure on dressing for tonight's game, Babe. I will ask Coach Harmon to take your name out of the lineup. I'm sorry, but you don't deserve to play."

Babe's jaw dropped. Stunned by what he had just heard, he looked pleadingly at Mr. Boswell.

"Oh no, sir. Tonight's game is a playoff game. If we win tonight, we will go to the regionals. Please don't make me sit out this game."

"You should have thought about that. As a team member, you are responsible to the rest of the team to use your head and set good examples for younger students to see."

"Mr. Boswell, I will do anything you ask me to do. I'll come in and do detention on Saturdays. I'll help clean the restrooms. Empty the trash. Anything! The team will need me tonight."

Babe's voice began to break. "Please, sir. I'm begging."

Mr. Boswell paused and looked at Babe intently. Then, probably only because he had once been an athlete and a former coach, he stepped back and said, "Okay, Babe, I'll give you grace on this, but no more monkey business, or I should say doggy business, the rest of the year. Do you understand?"

"Yes sir, thank you, sir," Babe replied. Relieved, Babe started to move away.

Mr. Boswell intervened.

"Two more things, Babe."

Babe took a step back. "Yes, sir."

"Make me know I made the right decision, okay? Not only in how you play tonight but how you comport yourself the rest of the school year. This school is an important asset to our community, and how the students act reflects the faculty and me. I will accept nothing short of excellence. Do you understand me, Babe?"

"Yes, sir. I do, and I'll do my best to make you proud. Thank you, Mr. Boswell. Babe paused a moment. "And um, the second thing?"

"You will report for detention Saturday morning at nine o'clock."

"Yes, sir!"

"Now, get out of here," Mr. Boswell said with a slight grin. "Before I change my mind."

Babe turned and double-timed it up the steps and into the school building before Mr. Boswell could do that.

The home team won a close game that night. When Babe came home from the gym, Dad, Mom, and Den were excited to hear his take on the game.

"Heck of a game, Babe," Dad said, putting his newspaper aside when Babe came through the door.

Den said, "Yeah, you played great, little brother." He stepped forward and gave Babe a shoulder hug. "You were knocking them down from outside. It looked like you were firing everybody up as well."

"Yeah, well, I felt pretty inspired tonight."

"So now we're in the regionals. The first time we've been there in a long time," Den added. "If we win there, we head to the state championship."

"What do you mean, 'if' we win?" Babe replied as he looked at his brother with a huge grin.

"Just trying to keep it real, Babe. Just trying to keep it real."

Mom remained quiet during the entire exchange but decided it was her turn to talk. "We're proud of both of you boys, but speaking of realism, don't you both have homework to do, including studying for upcoming English exams?"

Den laughed and said, "Aw, Mom, we ain't got no need to do no homework. Specially in English."

Dad ended the conversation by throwing one of his slippers toward the boys, "Get outta here, you two!"

* * *

One night toward the end of the school year, as we were propped up in bed, Babe showed me the class picture in the school yearbook.

"There you are," he said, pointing his finger at my picture. "I bet you are the only dog who ever had his picture taken for a high school yearbook, Speed. You could become famous over this." Then he paused for a moment and lowered his voice as he put his hand firmly on my head and made the following declaration: "So, by the powers vested in me by no particular entity, in recognition of your great contributions to the academic excellence of the class of '53, I, Babe, now, at this hallowed time and place, my bedroom, officially elevate you, Speed, into the historical records of Barrymore High School." Then he grabbed me around my neck and gave me a major hug. "Isn't that something? You are officially a Class of '53 Barrymore High School member. And we have the picture to prove it. Congratulations."

Then he tilted his head back and said, "I want you to know Mr. Boswell was so mad at me over this stunt that he almost kicked me off the team! He said we should not have a dog in our class picture. Can you believe that? I wanted to remind him we were the Barrymore Huskies. But I thought better of it. Besides, you aren't a husky. You are a plain old farm collie." He laughed aloud. "Just an old farm dog! That's what you are!" What a great night, what a great master I had.

That same night, as we snuggled together under the blankets, Babe whispered something I will never forget. "You are my best friend. I love you, Speed. Do you know what, buddy? We will always be together, you and me. We will even be in heaven together once we leave this earth. I promise you, Speed, heaven will be our home. I can promise you that because Jesus promised us when He said, 'Ask, and you will receive, knock, and the door will be open.' So, I asked Him to let you into heaven. That's what happened, Speed. I asked, and He answered. One thing for sure, Speed, God does not lie."

Love is a beautiful thing. The Bible says, "God is love." Of course, up here, love is everywhere. Heaven is a fabulous place for every creature who lives here. There is no sadness, sorrow, or pain in heaven. Life is perfect. And it's the home of the most important person who ever lived, Jesus Christ. He is my Master and Master to every believer. When I lived on Earth as a dog, Babe was my master. In the world and in heaven, Jesus is Master.

There is a beautiful verse in the Bible where Jesus says, "Behold, I stand at the door and knock. If anyone hears my voice and opens the door, I will dine with him and him with me." Jesus is speaking. He knocks on a believer's door. If that person answers, Jesus will come in and when the person dies, he will go to heaven.

And Babe told me many times, "If that person owns a dog, and if he asks, you can be certain, that dog will go to heaven too—especially if his name is Speed."

CHAPTER 11
DUMP REVISITED

The following winter in eastern Oregon was again frigid, with lots of snow. One night it snowed so hard that it was determined unsafe for the school buses to operate, so the school shut down. A few boys in Babe's class decided to spend the day sledding.

Five boys and I trudged up the road past Hogsback, where I once lived, beyond the city dump to a hillside that offered a steep slope. A heavy downfall had dumped about two feet of snow over the whole valley. County snowplows were out early, allowing farm families who lived in the foothills to get back and forth from their homes to wherever they needed to go. The boys were excited because it was a day away from school and a perfect day for sledding.

The sled run was long and quite steep. It was so steep that when the boys took off, they got to the bottom in just minutes unless they ran off the road, which happened often. I ran up and down several times until I got bored. After that, I just hung out at the bottom and greeted the sledders when they finished the run. It wasn't long before I got bored with that.

Part of the problem was a nagging temptation to wander back to the city refuse dump and see what might be new since I was last there. I had not been near the dump since Big's tragic death. Hogsback, Big, our struggle for food, and the city dump had played meaningful roles in my life at one time, and I had a compelling urge to go back and renew those memories. Besides, it was still early in the afternoon, and the boys were having such a fun time I knew they wouldn't miss me. So, I yielded and turned back—back down the road to my past.

As the dump came into view and the smells grew richer, I saw that the landfill had grown considerably. There was more of everything: old cars, tires, and helter-skelter piles of furniture and appliances. This abundance of junk was a sure indication that the populace in the surrounding valley was ever-increasing.

The caretaker's trailer house was still there, but it was deeper into the center of the dump than before. I could tell someone was still living there because I could see smoke from the chimney and hear noises inside. I sidled around to the south end of the dump and made my way to the area where I had said goodbye to Big. I hated what I saw—several months of bulldozer work pushing and leveling the landfill around left me nothing but a view of trash on top of more trash. His burial site was gone. I looked anxiously but had no idea where Big's body could be.

Finally, I just picked a spot and lay down. My mind and heart flooded with memories of Big, our times together, and how much I missed him. I was troubled that Big had never found his own master as I had. His life would have been so different. He would have been an ideal partner for a human to have.

I don't know how long I lay there, but I suddenly realized I needed to return to Babe and his friends before they came looking for me. Unfortunately, just as I stood up and took my first steps to loop around to the north, I heard the storm door of the trailer house squeak open. I stopped and crouched, watching the trailer as the caretaker stepped onto the porch. Yes, he was the same man who killed Big three years ago. He was wearing a shabby, dark, hooded wool coat he undoubtedly found in his front yard. Once again, I caught the scent of the same aroma I had experienced a few years ago as two men sat on the bed of a pick-up truck, discussing my worth as they passed a liquor bottle back and forth between them.

Deep anguish suddenly surged through my body when the caretaker closed the door behind himself. I watched this man stand and proudly exult over his domain of garbage and junk. At first, an intense hatred overcame me, but it didn't last long. Surprisingly, I began to feel a slight sense of sympathy for the man. He was as lonesome for companionship as I once was before Babe came into my life. Had he lost his little dog? That mean thought initially delighted me, but only for a minute because I began to hear the little guy yipping and scratching at the door to get outside. The man turned and reopened his door, and out popped a fiery ball of fur that weighed no more than twenty pounds. The dog exploded off the porch before the caretaker could scoop him up. He shot through the open gate, down the steps, and headed straight for me.

"Rascal! Get back here," the caretaker screamed as he leaned over the rail on his porch. Rascal paid no attention. He was on a mission. A strange animal had invaded his territory, and he would not stand for that!

I had no idea how he caught my scent amid all the surrounding smells in that place, but he did, and he was barking his fool head off as he squirmed his way over and around piles of garbage, broken concrete blocks, and cardboard boxes filled with who knows what. I didn't know what to do, so I did nothing. That was a mistake because Rascal was all over me in a flash. He started right for my face, neck, and ears, sinking his sharp teeth into any part of me not protected by my thick winter fur coat.

Of course, I was unhappy about this, so I grabbed him by the scruff of his neck and tossed him against an old rusty wheelbarrow. Unfazed, my aggressor ripped off a screeching howl and was right back in my face, slashing and tearing at my nose and ears again. At the same time, I was aware of the fast-approaching hulk of the caretaker, rifle in hand, bearing down on the two of us. At that point, I knew I had to get out of there and fast before I met the same fate Big had suffered at the hands of this trigger-happy junk man.

As the caretaker dodged in and out of the trash piles, I shook Rascal loose and bounded away. Rascal started right back after me vigorously, grabbing my right back leg and clamping down. I immediately pulled him off and dove out of sight. At that moment, the caretaker tripped over a half-buried bed rail and fell forward. As the man hit the ground, his rifle exploded, and immediately, Rascal let out an earsplitting howl and pitched head over heels into the remains of a water-soaked and filthy mattress.

I didn't stick around to see what followed, but Rascal had a large hole in his little body, with blood spilling from the wound. As I slipped away, I could hear the caretaker crying. "Rascal, oh no. Rascal! Rascal!" I didn't look back, but Rascal must have died in his master's arms that day. There was no way he could have survived that gunshot wound.

I might have been happy, relishing a vengeful victory over what the caretaker had done to me years before. But I wasn't. I knew the man loved his little dog, and his dog was dead. Never mind that this same man had killed my best friend. Dogs are forgiving animals, and I had long ago forgiven him. I could not imagine how terrible he felt, knowing his actions caused the death of his best friend. I didn't want to think how Babe would have suffered had it been us. The bond between a dog and his master is deep and forever. Separation from my master was unthinkable under any circumstances. I would never let that happen!

* * *

Babe entered the eleventh grade that year. His days were long because he played three major sports: football, basketball, and baseball. Babe had a practice of some kind after school every day. I greeted him after every practice when he rounded the corner of the red barn. We still had fun together, though our opportunities were fewer. Babe learned to drive that year, so he could use the family car, but only on rare occasions. He had to share those times with Den in his senior year. There was only one car, and Dad had priority. Den was second in line because Mom didn't drive. Babe was at the bottom of the pecking order, which was fine. I wasn't crazy about the car because it always took someone away from home.

It became clear that Babe was becoming a young man that school year. Quality time together grew more infrequent as the months passed. Even with his time at school and ball practice, my Babe-time seemed more disproportionate than ever. Babe was away from home more, and when he was at home, he seemed to have his mind on anything but me. He would often lie on his bunk bed and stare at the ceiling for prolonged periods. I would be up there with him, but it didn't matter. He was lost in thought as he seemed to drift into a different world than the one we shared. Why?

Then one day, it dawned on me—JOAN. She was the problem. I figured it out when they showed up at the house one night. They drove up in Dad's car, and I saw him put his arms around her and give her a big kiss right on the lips. They sat in the car for a long time, hugging and kissing before getting out and walking up the porch steps. I was on the porch, wagging my tail like crazy.

"Hey buddy," he said as he reached down, scratched my ears, and patted me. Yes, he did take a minute to pat me on the head as they walked by, but that was it. I certainly didn't get the love Joan got. His arm was around her the whole time. He never took his eyes off the girl.

What is going on here? All I get is a quick pat on the head. Come on, Babe!

Of course, I was happy to get the pat on the head, but a significant hug would have been a lot better. Or a "Good boy, Speed." Anything! But it wasn't to be. As for the girl, all I got from her was a cutesy smile as she reached for the door handle.

I lay down on the porch and waited for them to return. The lovebirds remained inside the house for a long time, but eventually, they did come out. Mom and Dad came out as well. Mom said, "You kids, be careful now. Remember, Babe, home by eleven, okay?"

"Yes, Mom. Don't worry, and you don't need to wait up for me."

"I won't wait up, Babe. But I will be awake until I hear you come home. You do know that, don't you?"

"Yeah, Mom. I know."

"Good. Good night, Joan. Tell your folks hello from us, please."

"I will," Joan smiled. "Good night."

I watched as they got back in the car and drove away. I didn't even get a pat on the head or a "see you later" on that trip. Babe was too busy helping his girlfriend get down the steps and into the car.

* * *

Den was now a senior in high school, which was important for him and all the family. He was in the spotlight most of the year. He was a football star, which made everyone proud. Den and Babe were close. They would get into an argument occasionally, but I only recall one time when things got serious between them. They were both competitive, especially when it came to sports.

One summer afternoon, they played a pick-up football game on the empty lot near our house. They played these games without protective pads and were rough at times.

In this game, Babe and Den were on opposite sides. The competition was intense, and on one play, Babe and Den got into a shoving match which didn't go well for Babe. It started when Den crashed into Babe after throwing a long pass to Dale.

"That's roughing the passer," Babe screamed into Den's face as he got to his feet.

"You're crazy. It was a fair hit. Get out of my face!" With that, he shoved Babe to the ground.

Babe jumped up and took a wild swing at his brother, aiming for the side of his head but getting air. Den calmly stepped toward Babe and, pointing at his chin, said, "Go ahead, Babe. Take your best shot, but don't expect me to turn the other cheek."

I didn't know what to do. I didn't like what was going on between these two, but all I could do was bark, which I did several times as they stood there glaring at one another. I wanted to protect Babe, but I couldn't go after Den. I was in a great dilemma.

Finally, Dale stepped in between the two boys and said, "Come on, guys. Let's take a break." With that, the game was over. Some of the boys wandered away toward town while Dale, Babe, and I moved to our front yard and sat on the grass. Den went inside the house.

* * *

Many things were going on that spring, especially in preparation for Den's graduation from high school. Den also had a girlfriend, so between the two boys' social lives and the graduation, I, being a mere dog, was an afterthought at best. I managed it because I loved my family with all my heart. They could do no wrong as far as I was concerned.

When graduation day arrived, the whole family came to Barrymore to honor the graduate. I received much attention from the several grandkids present. It was fun but short-lived. Ken and his family were there, without Kilroy. Wallace, on leave from the Marines, was there. Everyone was proud of Den, who would leave for college in the fall. As I said, it didn't last long. In just a few days, they had all departed.

It was a different kind of summer for our family. Weird, even. Dale was gone. He enlisted in the Navy right after high school. I missed Dale, and I know Babe did too. There were too few fishing trips. Summer came and quickly left. Babe spent his free time with Joan, which was a waste. Fergie continued to avoid me. Oddly, no one noticed or cared about these things except me. Over time, my status declined to the "family dog."

When September arrived, Den left for college, and Babe was the only boy left at home. Life became quieter, but more complicated. Babe, on occasion, did find time to spend with me. We would get in the car and drive around town or go on long drives in the country. I always occupied the front seat next to Babe. He would crank the window down on my side for me to enjoy the autumn air as we drove through the valley. In the late summer, you could smell the aroma of the fresh bales of hay stacked in the fields waiting to be loaded into hay barns or onto hay trucks to go to markets nearby.

I loved the smell of mature mint, peas, corn, potatoes, and onions. Of course, I could also smell the residue of the nearby cattle and horse farms. Quite often, Babe would stop the car on a high ridge near Horseshoe Bend, and we would get out of the car and stretch our legs. Barrymore was a small town, but it shone beautifully and peacefully from that vantage point, like a beautiful pearl resting in the middle of a lush river valley.

You could see smoke rising from the sawmills that populated the area. These mills provided livelihoods for the families who lived there. Across the horizontal landscape, you could see mile after mile of the graceful Grand Ronde River as it snaked along the east side of town, heading north to join the Wallowa River and eventually flowing into the mighty Snake River in western Idaho.

One time, as we sat on that overlook viewing our beautiful valley together, I remember Babe putting his arm around me and saying, "Next year, Speed, I'll be gone a lot. But you'll be okay. Mom and Dad will take good care of you while I'm gone. And when I graduate from college, I'll return to Barrymore to live. We'll get us a place, you and me, Speed. Just the two of us. Won't that be great?" He pulled me in close and gave me kisses. I kissed him back. I wanted to stay there with Babe forever. Just the two of us, my master and me, together forever.

CHAPTER 12
HEAD OVER HEELS

Thereere were complications when Babe began his final year in high school. One of them you already know about—Joan. Things didn't improve on that front, at least from my perspective. Babe was with Joan whenever he was not at school or at an athletic event. And whenever she was not around, he would slip into his world of dopiness and become non-communicative. For the life of me, I could not understand it. How could a person, especially a girl, cast such a spell on a super-intelligent being? This phenomenon remained a constant mystery as I watched the back-and-forth between Babe and Joan play out.

I languished in this cluelessness until one eventful fall evening when Queen Bee appeared. I had no idea where she came from or to whom she belonged. I did not know her real name or her pedigree. All I can say is that she suddenly and mysteriously popped into our yard and into my life from nowhere.

And, I might add, she was the most beautiful creature I had ever seen.

This lady was perfect in every detail. She wore soft, sable fur coat rich in color. She owned a set of deep-set, vigilant brown eyes, freckled front legs, short, pointed ears that drooped at the top, a cute, provocative tail, and a picture-perfect, moist, jet-black nose. She was a knockout!

Queen Bee was slightly smaller than I was, with a little more of a tapered torso. Near perfect by any measure. And she knew how to flirt, big-time! I was sitting on the ledge of our front porch when here she came, prancing up the street like a high-stepping drum major leading a brass band in a grand parade.

She was by herself, however, following her nose, which led her right to my food dish. She strutted onto our front yard, across our driveway, and up the porch steps. Then she planted her beautiful black nose into my half-filled plate of dog food and proceeded to eat my dinner. I could not believe what I was seeing.

Hey, what is going on with you? Who do you think you are anyway? Get out of here!

At least, that is the message I wanted to convey, but I couldn't. All I could do was sit there, try to control my tail, and stare at this impertinent pooch as she ate my dinner. Occasionally, she looked at me, blinked her eyes once or twice, and then returned to my dinner.

Finally, I'd had enough of that and jumped off the porch ledge. In a matter of seconds, we were nose-to-nose in my food dish. The very first thing I learned about this lady was that she was no—well, no lady. She looked at me out of the corner of her eye, curled back her upper lip, emitted an unladylike nasty growl, and returned to my dinner. Due to her incivility, I decided the best thing for me to do was to sit down and think about things for a while. I was nervous as I sat there and watched her lick my plate clean before mischievously pushing it over to me with a sassy wink.

That did it! At that moment, I knew I was in love! I was head-over-heels in love, and it was immediate and irreversible! But I did not have time to dwell on that predicament because suddenly, Ms. Queen Bee bounded off the porch and headed back across the driveway. I gave chase, and when I caught up to her, we engaged in a harmless mock fight in our front yard before I chased her in hot pursuit around the house several times. Occasionally, we interrupted the chase game and challenged one another in a fierce, spoofy battle. These battles would last until we were exhausted and had to get some air and slow down our heart rates. I wasn't sure if my heart was beating as much from the frolicking as it was for this beautiful new animal. I was in a new world, and I never wanted it to end.

It was a fabulous moment, and Queen Bee loved it too. In that time-out, we were content to lie on the grass and stare at one another, waiting for the other to make the next move and start the second stanza of our incredible romantic overture.

Who is this creature? Where did she come from, and where does she live? Is this just a dream from which I'll suddenly awaken and find myself alone again in my yard, waiting for Babe to come home? I hope not. And if it is, please don't wake me up.

Queen Bee was not her real name, but it defined her. I'm not sure how long we lay there, but it began to get dark. There were now twinkling stars above, joined by a bright crescent moon. A cool summer breeze eased in, making the evening even more magical.

I couldn't take my eyes off this beautiful creature. As I lay there, I kept asking myself, *What is happening to me? Does this beauty have a family? If not, how can I keep her? Protect her? Own her?* My mind was racing as fast as my heart. There were no answers. All I knew was this little lady was DRIVING ME CRAZY!

I finally got to my feet and walked around to her other side, behind where she lay. She didn't look up or even raise an ear in my direction. I barked at her several times, thinking that would draw her notice. But it didn't. She lay there, pretending to be asleep, even though I knew she was wide awake and playing a lover's game with me.

As we lay there, something that had suddenly been a mystery and source of intense irritation to me was no longer a mystery. My current euphoria was no different than what Babe was experiencing in his relationship with Joan. I understood and appreciated what was happening to him better. Those times he was so silent, staring at nothing and saying little, finally made sense.

Occasionally, we bounced to our feet, growling and enticing one another into another round of play. The stars were out, and the moon's light highlighted her coat, causing her to glow in the dark. I did not want this evening to end.

Finally, Babe returned home from a date with Joan. He pulled the car onto the driveway and opened the garage door. I jumped up and went over to greet him. Queen Bee didn't move. She lay there and looked at Babe as he hugged me and rubbed my neck. Then he looked over and saw my new friend.

He said, "What have we here?" Babe and I walked over to Queen Bee. She immediately sat up, wagged her tail, cocked her head, and gave Babe a welcoming look. Babe dropped to his knees, delivered her tender pats, and rubbed around her neck and ears. Queen Bee liked that and began wagging her tail with enthusiasm.

"What is your name, little girl?" Queen Bee gave Babe four or five wet licks on his hands. They hit it off immediately, which made me feel good!

"Do you belong to someone, little lady? You have a collar on. Let me look at it, okay?" He lifted his index finger under the collar to see it better. Queen Bee had a fair amount of fur around her neck, and it was now dark outside. Babe leaned in as far as he could but couldn't read the inscription plate.

"Well, it's too dark to read tonight, little girl. We will have to wait until tomorrow. That is, if you're still around by tomorrow." He stood and, for a moment, looked at me, then back at Queen Bee. "So, what do you say, Speed? Are you coming in the house with me tonight, or will you spend the night out here with your new friend?" Sensing my dilemma, he paused for a minute, then added, "Up to you, buddy." He paused momentarily, then started for the back door. Halfway there, he turned back to me. "Are you coming?"

I was in a real quandary at that point. I always slept with Babe, but now I feared Queen Bee would not stick around until morning. That would be unacceptable. So, I moved close to Queen Bee and sat down beside her. Babe smiled and turned back toward the door. "Okay, pal. Suit yourself. I'll see you in the morning." He opened the door and disappeared into the house.

I had mixed emotions about all of this, but I hoped Babe might now know how I felt when he often rejected me in favor of Joan. I thought I did the right thing at the time, and I still do today. Anyway, Queen Bee and I spent the night roaming the neighborhood. I even took her to Hogsback and showed her where I lived before coming to Babe's family.

We sat side by side that night on the edge of a flat precipice as the full moon brightened the sky. I sensed feelings within myself I had never felt before. As we snuggled together through the night, I knew she shared those feelings in my heart. We were in love.

Toward morning, we came back down the hill and strolled through town. We had no agenda. We were just enjoying our time together. Barrymore was quiet and peaceful. Most of my friends were off the streets, which I was happy about since I had no intention of sharing Queen Bee with anyone, human or animal.

By the time we got back home, the sun had already risen. I could hear Mom puttering over breakfast for Dad and Babe, and it wasn't long before Babe popped his head out, probably to see if we were both still there. When he saw us, he came outside and walked over to where Queen Bee was lying.

"Hey, little lady. How are you this morning?" He crouched down beside her and again put his hand under her collar. He smiled and looked at me. "Guess what, Speed. Your friend's name is Kate, and she has a phone number on her collar. Let me go inside and see if I can find out who Kate belongs to."

With that, Babe stood and walked back to the house. I was unsure what was happening, but I knew if Babe handled things, all would be well. I looked at Kate and lay down beside her. In a short time, Babe was back, grinning broadly. He knelt between Kate and me and gave us equal head and neck rubs.

"I have good news, guys. Kate's family lives less than five miles away. How about that! It looks like you all will be able to see each other again."

Mom soon joined us.

She asked, "What did you find out, son?"

Babe replied, "Well, I called the number on her collar and found out the little lady's name is Kate. She belongs to the Greer family, who moved here recently from Washington state."

"Oh, that's the family who bought the Mason farm a few months ago."

"Right. Mrs. Greer said she would come down and pick Kate up, but I told her it would be no problem for us to put her dog in the car and bring her out there."

"Good, that way we can make some new friends. I'll go inside and see if I can find a few cupcakes and cookies to take over to them."

"Hmmm, that sounds good," Babe answered.

Moments later, Babe, Mom, Kate, and I were in the car and on our way to Kate's house. The trip wasn't long, just a short drive north of town. Kate and I jumped out of the car when Babe opened the door. We soon stood in Kate's front yard, waiting for Babe and Mom to catch up. Kate's mom came out the front door just as Babe and Mom arrived. The folks introduced themselves, stood around for several minutes, and got acquainted. Kate and I romped around the yard, having a fun time. My intuition told me Kate and I would have a special relationship, and my intuition was right on target.

CHAPTER 13
FAMILY MATTERS

Babe's final year in school was fast approaching, but we managed to squeeze in one final late-summer overnight fishing trip. Our fishing experiences were not the same without Dale, but they were still fun. There were still plenty of rainbow trout in Indian Creek, and those nights outside with a friendly fire to cook our fish and keep us warm were incredible.

I often wished I could have brought Kate along so she could see the special bond Babe and I shared, but I knew something like that would come together by chance rather than by design.

One of these trips began early on a gorgeous June morning. Babe decided to make this an overnighter on Indian Creek. Instead of coming home at the end of the day, we would spend the night. He packed his sleeping bag and a camping kit, including a frying pan, plastic cups, and plates, and off we went. We fished all day, moving up and down the creek. Babe did the fishing, and I chased everything that moved.

Babe cleaned his catch in the creek that night. Then he gathered some twigs and branches from nearby fallen tree limbs and started a small fire, making sure it was well protected from spreading. In a few minutes, Babe had a nice little blaze going. Then he crouched near the fire and looked over at me.

"Are you ready for dinner, boy? We have fresh trout here and some potato salad you will not like. But don't worry, buddy. I also brought a package of your favorite snacks. How does that sound, my friend?"

With that, Babe set about preparing the fish for cooking. Mom had fixed him a bottle of olive oil, a small bag of flour, and some other seasoning and spices, which smelled good. I could hardly wait to start eating because I loved the taste of trout, and we had plenty. I had no interest in the dog food. Babe carefully removed the bones from the fish so we would not have a problem with those pesky things. Anyway, it was a delicious meal. I loved every part of it, even the potato salad.

We lay out under God's heavens that night. There was no tent, just a warm sleeping bag where we could cuddle. The stars blinked at us while we surveyed their enormous expanse. It was a unique experience I will never forget.

Babe talked about how God had made the sun, the stars, and the moon. I thank God for His wonderful creation, the fish and the plants, the farm animals, the birds, and all the stars we saw that night. God created us, too, and He watched over us as we slept that night.

Babe repeated an important truth that night as we cuddled together. He said, "We will always be together, Speed, even after we leave this earth. God has prepared a place in heaven for both of us. I know it is beautiful here, but it will be even more so in heaven. And we will be there forever. I asked God for you to be there with me, Speed, and because I prayed for that, you can believe it will happen. God answers prayers, Speed. I know He does."

Holding his Bible near the light of the fire, Babe read these words to me: "If you abide in me, and my words abide in you, ask whatever you wish, and it will be done for you." Then Babe propped himself on one elbow and softly stroked my neck and back. It was a perfect evening. What a loving master I had. And at the time, I could not imagine heaven being any better than where we were that night. But now that I have been here, I can assure you that heaven is a perfect place. I cannot wait to share it with Babe.

Babe's final year in school began in September. It promised to be a busy one. However, our football team didn't do well that fall, finishing the season with only three wins. Babe was disappointed, of course, but even worse, he suffered a broken collar bone toward the end of the season, so football ended that year on a sour note.

Basketball was better. We won the league championship and played for the state championship in Oregon's state capitol, Salem. And even though our team lost the championship game, it was a proud moment for the school and town to have reached the finals in the state championship tournament.

Soon, spring baseball would start, and the fish would be biting. Lots of excitement still lay ahead. Spring was always the most fun time, with another fantastic eastern Oregon summer to follow. No worries—except for the loss of a family member. I was aware we hadn't seen Fergie for several days. This cat and I had our issues, but we had learned to live together. The fact that she had not shown up for a while was odd, so I decided to look for her.

First, I checked inside the woodshed where her dish was. It was there, full of food. I was not fond of cat food, so I passed by it. The building had no fresh scent of Fergie. I searched through the narrow space between the woodshed and the fence around the yard next to us. There was no sign of Fergie there, so I decided to explore the area behind Dale's house, which stretched out a long way before ending at the property owned by the Borden family. This older couple had lived there for ten or so years. I reached the end of that fence line without catching any scent belonging to Fergie.

It was odd I felt obligated to find this cat, even though she had humbled and embarrassed me when we first met. I decided to expand my search to a larger area encompassing several city blocks, including a few miles up the mountain road to the Blue Mountains. After an hour of intense searching and sniffing for signs of Fergie, I considered heading east through town and over the bridge leading toward Horseshoe Bend, but I decided against that because I had never seen her come from that direction and could see no reason she would have gone east. So, after spending several hours looking, I was tired and decided to chuck it in and head for home. I did so with great reluctance because I knew something bad must have happened to Fergie to cause her to stay away for so long. I resolved to find her, no matter what.

* * *

One day Babe and I were on our way home from a downtown Barrymore visit, where we had been socializing with friends, when Babe called me to a poster on a telephone pole.

"Look here, Speed."

I cocked my head and looked at the poster. I saw a picture of Babe and another young man. They were glaring at each other.

"I know you can't read it, but I'll tell you about it, okay? It says, 'SLIDE TROMBONE BLOWOUT—WHO'S THE BEST IN THE VALLEY?' and it's a picture of Martin and me holding our trombones against a large sheet of music. It's all about the big blowout contest at our spring concert. Our band director came up with the harebrained idea that Martin and I would compete for the title of the best trombonist in the Grande Ronde Valley, Martin or me. Do you get it, Speed?"

I looked at the picture again and then cocked my head, looked back at Babe, and at the picture again. "This contest will help sell more tickets to the concert," he said. "Guaranteed! He has posted these silly things all over the valley."

It took some effort because my sight wasn't nearly as good as my sense of smell, but I did recognize Martin. The boys were friends, but also rivals at times. They would sometimes get together in our yard and practice basketball or throw a baseball back and forth. Martin was a great athlete—the best in the whole school, actually. He was the ace pitcher on our baseball team, as well as the captain of the football team. Not only that, but Martin was our top scorer in basketball. In addition to all those accomplishments, Martin was the senior class president. With all those things going for him, Martin was, understandably, the most popular boy in the whole school.

Babe studied the poster for several minutes. I could sense he was stressed. Then he slowly dropped to one knee, put his arm around my neck, and spoke softly with conviction, "I've got to win this contest!" Then he put his mouth to my ear and whispered, "Martin will win the 'Best Athlete' award and he deserves to win it, no question. But here's my problem, Speed. The contest winner will likely win the annual band award, the only award I have a chance to win. So, there you have it, Speed. If Martin wins this, he walks away with two of the three most prestigious senior awards."

There was a long, thoughtful pause, followed by a normal tone. "Doggone it, Speed. I should not be envious, but Martin is our senior class president, student council president, and the most popular kid in school."

He went silent for a few minutes as we began to walk again.

Then, suddenly, he stopped again. He knelt, pulled me in close, and in a low voice said, "Here's the kicker, Speed. I haven't told you this. He has even asked Joan if she would go out with him. Can you believe that? This guy could date any girl in school, but he wants to date my girl!"

We walked on, and Babe was quiet for a long while. Finally, he stopped one last time, looked up at the sky, and yelled at the top of his voice, "I'VE GOT TO WIN THIS CONTEST!!"

* * *

The next few weeks were very dull. Whenever Babe was not in school, he was home practicing his trombone, preparing for the big event. Of course, I was with him in the same room at first. But after hearing Babe practice the song he had chosen over and over again, I became weary and relocated to the front porch.

I also took an occasional side trip to the country to visit Kate whenever possible.

When the night of the band concert finally arrived, Babe put on his only suit and left the house on foot, trombone case in hand. Mom and Dad followed an hour later, leaving me at home. They all seemed quite nervous, just like before an important ball game. And even though I couldn't attend, I am able to relay to you every detail of that evening's magic event.

Hundreds of townspeople poured into the high-school auditorium. The band got things started by playing well-known tunes, lively but not loud, soothing to the ear, but nothing exciting. However, an underlying tension brought about by the hype of the upcoming contest began to creep in, causing a slight feeling of uneasiness throughout the auditorium.

The two competitors, Babe and Martin, sat opposite one another at the front of the stage.

Finally, Conductor Hagerty stepped to the center stage between the boys.

"Ladies and gentlemen, the time you all have been waiting for has finally arrived. We are excited to present tonight two young men who excelled in their musical abilities in the high school band for several years—even before they were in high school, for that matter. And tonight, you will have the opportunity to see and hear them display their talents as they perform in this friendly competition we have labeled 'Slide Trombone Blowout.'"

He then introduced Babe and Martin and explained the details of the contest and the songs they would play. Babe had chosen a spirited march by John Philip Sousa, "On the Tramp," a fast-moving piece demanding a lot of action and skilled trombone musicianship. He was to perform first, as determined by a coin toss.

Babe was nervous. His knees wobbled a bit as he walked to center stage. But as he began to play, his confidence kicked in, and he could feel the tension easing. His body started to sway perfectly with the notes coming from his horn, and he could sense his entire body expressing the music. The many hours he had spent practicing for the event were paying great dividends. His body, the instrument, and the music were in perfect harmony. It was so sweet. His confident expression clearly showed he was in no hurry for his time in the limelight to end. But it did, and the audience exploded with resounding applause and a chorus of "Bravo!" and "Oh yeah!"

Grinning widely, Babe strode to the back of the stage and took his seat as first chair of the trombone section of the Barrymore High School Band. He was a proud young man. Babe had nailed it big time and knew it. He glanced at Martin, who graciously gave him a thumbs-up.

It was now Martin's turn. As he strode to center stage, Martin looked loose and relaxed. He was used to being in the spotlight. Martin's choice of music, "In The Mood," was an excellent trombone piece.

Martin started playing in slow, soft tones. Then gradually, he began to pick up the tempo and volume. In just minutes, Martin was jiving and romping around the entire stage, bending and twisting his tall body into weird shapes and contortions. He even jumped upon an empty chair at one point, blaring his horn so loud he tested the acoustics in the new auditorium. After performing a two-minute tap dance on the chair, Martin dropped to the floor, playing and grooving until the end of his song. He never missed a beat or hit a sour note. He was terrific and ended his performance with a slide on his knees to the front of the stage, thrusting his horn high in the air and screaming, "OH YEAH!"

Martin received a standing ovation as he returned to the rest of the band. Before he got to his chair, Babe's not-so-diplomatic friend Don leaned back to Babe from his seat in the trumpet section and whispered, "You're screwed!"

Even though there was no trophy or winner announcement that night, there was no doubt that Martin won the contest. Babe was deeply disappointed, of course. He fretted about it for several days, but finally realized Martin had the better performance and deserved to win.

* * *

Without a doubt, by far the most exciting thing that happened to me that year was when I learned I had a family of my own. Babe came out of the house one day and called me. He was excited and grinning from ear to ear. As always, I hurried over to where he was standing.

Are we going fishing?

He said, "Guess what, buddy?"

I cocked my head as he knelt, grabbed the scruff of my neck with both hands and started shaking me and laughing like crazy. He said, "Speed, you rascal. Now you've done it!"

He put his arms around my neck, pulled me in, and continued to laugh. "You're a daddy, man. You and Kate have a family of eight little puppies." He was excited. I didn't know what was so exciting, but because he was excited, I was too. We both started jumping up and down and dancing around. Then he shouted, "Come on! We have got to go see Kate." Of course, I was ready to go anywhere with Babe. We jumped in the car and took off to Kate's house.

Both Mrs. and Mr. Greer met us at the front door. Mr. Greer was wearing a State of Oregon police uniform. "They're around back," Mrs. Greer said. She led us around the house to a workshop in the backyard of Kate's home.

I could hear Kate's happy squeal followed by a sharp bark as we drew near the shop. Mrs. Greer opened the door, and we all stepped inside. I could not believe what I saw. It was amazing. Kate was lying on her bed, and eight squirming puppies were crawling all over her. Most of them didn't have their eyes open. Kate looked up at me.

"Come over and meet your babies, Daddy."

"My babies? These are my babies?"

"They are. You're a daddy now."

"Wow, Kate. I can't believe it."

"Aren't they beautiful?" Mrs. Greer said, as she proudly gestured toward the new family.

Babe knelt and softly started patting Kate's head. "They sure are," Babe said. He reached down, picked up one of the pups, and cradled it in his arms. Then he looked at me, "You did good, Speed. I'm proud of you, man."

Feeling overwhelmed, I ventured over and gave Kate a nose kiss. The little puppies tumbled all over her and her bed.

Babe put his arm around me. "Look here, Daddy. It's customary to pass out cigars on such occasions. You do realize that, don't you?"

Kate gave me an endearing look, which only added to my excitement. Babe stretched out his hand and patted her head.

"You're a mommy now, Kate. Eight little ones to look after. You're going to have your paws full." Kate gave Babe a look of total confidence as if to say, "No problem, Babe." She looked beautiful, and I was proud of her and strangely proud of myself. I now had my own family, which was not a bad accomplishment for a one-time cave-dwelling mutt.

"There are five girls and three boys," Kate's mom explained.

"Do you think you can find homes for them all?" Babe asked.

"I don't think that will be a problem," she answered.

Officer Greer, chiming in for the first time, said, "We'll want to keep one,"

Mrs. Greer looked at her husband and smiled. "Yes, he's already picked the one he wants to keep."

"Good," Babe replied. "My folks can help you find homes for the rest of them. I can put a note on our bulletin board at school. The kids all know Speed. More than likely, they will all want one."

Kate's mom laughed. "You're probably right about that. But we should wait a few weeks before we start that process. For starters, they should spend time with their mom."

"I get that. Just let me know."

"I will. But in the meantime, feel free to come by anytime and see how the puppies are doing. And you can bring Daddy along as well."

Babe laughed. "Yeah, just try to keep him away."

CHAPTER 14
PARTING WAYS

Soon, every plant was blooming on the hillsides and along the roadways. The glorious spring air was fresh and clean, with creeks and rivers flowing abundantly from the winter snowmelt. These were not the only blessings. It was baseball season! Great excitement abounded about the team's prospects of winning the state championship. Baseball had always drawn impressive turnouts from the hometown folks who faithfully showed up for home games. This year was the last for six of the players, including Babe.

The baseball team got off to a good start and was undefeated by mid-season. A game against Plymouth, a sizeable mid-state school, was the one everyone penciled in as a must-see game. I remember the eagerness in our house the night before Plymouth, also undefeated, came to town.

"They are an outstanding team, son," Dad said to Babe at the evening dinner table.

"Yeah, they are okay, I guess, but not as good as we are. They have a good pitcher, but Martin is better. Coach scouted them well. Their guy throws hard, and our coach says they have a couple of good hitters, but the rest of the team is not so great. We'll get our hits, don't worry. I predict we will knock him off the mound by the end of the third inning."

"You sound pretty cocky, young man."

"Just being honest, Dad. The way our clean-up batter has been hitting the ball, there are no worries, Dad."

"And your clean-up batter is?"

"That would be me."

Of course, I never knew any of the details or which games were essential. But I could feel the excitement each game day. I was going to be there. So were Dad and Mom and most of the town.

Babe had an excellent year going. He was hitting well and seemed to have a magic glove playing shortstop. The team was hot and rolling toward an undefeated season.

At the game, I sat beside Dad. We were behind the screen on the third-base side, close to the infield. The game moved along quickly, but by the fifth inning, I could tell by how our coach acted that our kids were not playing well. He displayed an unusual temper when he talked to his players, and he was constantly shouting at the two officials, dressed in black, who looked quite grim and did not seem to enjoy their jobs that day. The opposing players were trying to rough each other up by making unnecessary physical contact, and there was a lot of back-and-forth trash talk among the players. Our coach was quite upset, and the crowd seemed displeased as well. When a close call went against our team, the hometown crowd challenged the game officials with boos and other verbal abuse.

"Come on, Ump! That was not a strike! You're as blind as a bat!"

"He was out, Ump. Out by a mile. My eight-year-old could call a better game than you're calling! You are costing us this game. Come on, man!"

Babe was acting weird, not paying attention. At one point, late in the game, Babe sat on the bench, talking to his friend Don and writing stuff down. I learned later what was going on.

"Look here, Don. I just figured my batting average. I'm hitting close to four-fifty. Can you believe that?"

Don glanced at Babe's notes and said, "Yeah, well, you better forget that. That's history, man. This guy's throwin' strikes, and we haven't had a base hit all day. We've got a runner on second. You need to hit the ball and bring him home, Babe."

"No worries, Don," Babe replied. He stood up and picked up his bat. "I can do that."

Babe looked confident as he strode to the on-deck circle. He took some healthy practice swings and then stood and watched his teammate, usually a dependable hitter, go down after three straight strikes zipped past him and into the catcher's mitt. Babe walked to the plate. His coach called from near third base, "Come on, Babe. Be a hitter."

Babe smiled, nodded at the coach, knocked his bat against his cleats, wiped his hands on his jersey, and stepped up to the plate as he sucked in a lungful of air.

Dad hollered from behind the screen. "Keep your eye on the ball, Babe." I could also hear Mom cheer for her son from the bleacher section. I stood up and pressed against Dad's leg as he reached down and gently tapped my head. Babe's family was ready, Babe was ready, and I was ready.

Babe took two casual practice swings before assuming his stance at the plate. With his bat cocked near his right shoulder, he looked poised and comfortable. He stared at the big, left-handed pitcher, who was leaning forward, and waiting for a signal from the catcher, a hefty kid who popped his fist into his mitt with great authority.

"You got this guy's number, Michael," the catcher hollered to his pitcher. "Easy out."

At that, Babe turned his head, gave the catcher a smirky grin, then refocused on the pitcher. He had fouled out twice in earlier innings and knew he was due. This at-bat for Babe would be his moment to save the game for his team. He held the bat high, rotating it slightly while waiting for the first pitch. Michael went into his stretch, looked at the runner on second base, kicked his right leg high, and threw a fastball that rocketed across the middle of the plate and slammed into the catcher's mitt. POW!

"Strike!" came the call from the umpire.

"Good stuff, Michael. This guy can't see, let alone hit the ball," the catcher yelled as he zipped the ball back to Michael.

Babe stepped back and turned toward the coach.

"You've got this, Babe, come on," the coach encouraged. "A base hit is all we need."

Babe wiped his hands on his pants and stepped back to the plate, assuming his hitter's position. Once again, Michael leaned forward from his position on the mound. He was a tall kid, and his presence was imposing as he patiently waited for the catcher's signal. Several seconds passed as Michael didn't like what the catcher was offering, made known by quick head shakes. Finally, he got the sign he wanted, straightened up, and stood tall on the mound, taking his time before delivering the pitch.

Babe tensed up, ready for the ball to rocket out of the pitcher's hand.

The crowd grew fidgety over the delay and began to increase their cheering. I could hear them calling out to Babe with great enthusiasm. Babe was ready. When the pitcher finally launched his second pitch, Babe took a mighty swing and made solid contact with the ball. It looked good. The crowd roared as the ball came off Babe's bat.

Babe started his run toward first base as he and everybody else watched the ball sail down the left field line and out of play, landing in the back seat of a Ford convertible parked alongside the street next to the ball field.

"Foul ball," the umpire hollered.

It was not hard to hear the moans of the disappointed crowd or to see the disappointment on Babe's face as he picked up his bat and returned to the plate.

The catcher removed his mask and stepped out in front of home plate. He held up two fingers and called to his teammates, "Two outs! One more, right here." Then he returned to his position behind the plate and hollered to his pitcher, "Okay, Michael. Two strikes. We've got this guy. Show him some juice."

Once again, Michael took a lot of time getting ready to throw his third pitch. He went into his stretch, carefully studied the runner on second base, and then locked his eyes on Babe, who was crouched and ready. The stands were eerily quiet as Michael drew his left arm back and threw another rocket down the middle of the plate. Babe liked what he saw and took a healthy swing, making solid contact with the ball. This time the ball went deep into center field, but it landed straight into the waiting glove of the Plymouth center fielder, ending the inning.

Babe's head was down as he returned to the team bench. He picked up his glove and trotted onto the field. The home team had suffered its first season loss when the game was over. And sadly, things got worse for Babe.

He went the rest of the season without getting a base hit. His moment of pride was a good but costly lesson. He learned from it.

"I guess God was trying to teach me something," Babe whispered one night after the baseball season ended. We snuggled in bed together, having our quiet moments as we always did at the end of the day. "At least that's what my dad told me. I was so proud of how well I was hitting the ball that I let it go to my head. So, I got what I deserved. I was full of pride instead of honoring God and thanking Him for everything. The Bible tells us that we should do all we do for the glory of God. I was looking for my own glory, Speed. I know that's what happened. God let me know I messed up by not allowing me to get a hit the rest of the season. I won't make that mistake again, Speed. I can assure you of that."

I remember that night so well. Babe propped himself up on one elbow and began to pat my head and neck softly. He said, "I should be more like you, Speed. You're a perfect model for me to follow. You always try to please me. You never assume anything for yourself. You are happy when I'm happy, sad when I'm sad, and you are loyal to me, no matter what I do."

Babe pulled me up to his face and looked deeply into my eyes. "I want to learn to love my Master like you love me, Speed. With you, it's so natural. Do you think you could teach me to do that, Speed? I'm serious. I need to follow your lead, buddy."

That was a happy moment for us both. The conversation could have stopped right there, but Babe continued talking. He said, "I wish I could play summer ball this year, Speed, but I can't. For one thing, I'll have to work to go to college. But mostly because I want to spend more time with Joan. You know what I mean, don't you, Speed?" He laughed when he said this. Of course, I could only sense what he was talking about then. At the mention of Joan's name, I knew he was thinking about her. Now I could understand how he felt. Many of my thoughts centered around Kate and how much I loved her. Still, I knew Kate wasn't my life. Babe was.

* * *

After graduation, Babe took a summer job in one of the manufacturing plants in town. He worked in an area where they made wooden window coverings. He would catch a ride to work each morning with one of his friends, so I would not see him until he got home each night. Some of those nights, Babe and his folks sat at the kitchen table and engaged in serious discussions where they had pens and writing pads out and did lots of figuring and writing.

I didn't know what was happening then, which was good because I would have been brokenhearted had I known.

Babe and his folks discussed his college education away from home at a major university. In addition, his folks had decided to move to the southern coast of Oregon, a long distance away. Again, I was totally in the dark about all of that. But as the summer days clicked off, Babe was spending increased time with Joan and less time with me. When he was not working, he was out with her. With Den in college, Babe was number two in automobile rights, and he certainly took advantage of those opportunities.

Of course, the more time Babe spent with Joan, the less he had for me. I no longer felt any ill will toward her over this. I could understand it. I know she made him happy; my master's happiness was essential.

One Sunday after church, Babe and his parents invited Joan for dinner. Everyone was excited because she had never had a formal dinner with us. As the time was approaching when Babe would be leaving for college, this would be a significant get-together for the family. Mom even stayed home from church that morning to prepare the meal.

Babe and Joan walked home from church that Sunday, hand in hand. They were talking. I was running alongside. When they reached the red barn, Babe stepped into the shadow of the large building and pulled Joan up to him. It was a beautiful cool morning, quiet with only the sounds of the song sparrows and occasional American robins hovering above from the branches of the ponderosa pine trees that grew in the neighborhood.

They stood together quietly for precious minutes. Finally, Babe said, "This will be one of our last times to do this. I'm going to miss you, dear girl."

Joan looked into Babe's eyes. "Not as much as I will miss you, Babe."

"I'm going to miss everything about you, Joanie. Everything!" He pulled her body in close to his. "I want you to wait for me, darling. I'll do my best to get back here whenever I can."

After embracing in a tender silence for several minutes, Joan pushed back from Babe and looked back into his eyes, forcing herself to say, "That won't be possible, Babe."

"What do you mean?" Babe uttered.

"Think about it, Babe. Your folks are moving, remember?"

"Yeah, I know."

"It's a different day now, Babe. You'll be making new friends in college and trying to keep your grades up. On Thanksgiving and Christmas, you will need to be with your family. You won't be coming to Barrymore. Then, when summer comes, will you come to Barrymore to live or go to where your folks are in southern Oregon?"

Babe paused; he had no answer. He gave Joan a look of anguish and could only produce one word. "But…"

Joan took Babe's hand, "Do you understand what I'm saying, Babe? I'll be a senior in high school. We're too young to commit to one another. We need to trust God. He will make it happen if He wants us to get together later. If He doesn't, well, we will have beautiful memories."

Babe's stature sagged. His face paled. I didn't know what Joan said, but I could tell Babe was profoundly hurt and confused. He looked off into the distance over Joan's shoulder for a moment, then down at his feet for a few seconds, then at the sky, and then back at Joan.

Finally, he said, "I can't believe this is happening, Joan. We've always been together. Ever since eighth grade. I've prayed every day that God would keep us together."

Joan reached out and took Babe's hand. "Babe, of all the boys I know, you're the best. Your faith walk has been an inspiration to me and to everyone who knows you. But you know, Babe, we know so little about life. We have lived in this little town of fifteen hundred people our whole lives. There's a big world out there, Babe. Making lifetime promises to each other at our ages would be foolish. Don't you want to put everything in God's hands and let Him direct your steps? That's what I want. And that's what I want for you too. At such a crucial time, we need to trust God."

Babe looked at his beloved girlfriend and said, "I know you're right. It's just that I can't stand the thought of you dating someone else. It breaks my heart to think about that, Joan."

"Then you should have no worries. No one will want to date me, anyway." Joan picked up a stick and threw it about twenty feet ahead. "Fetch, Speed."

Babe laughed. "He doesn't do 'fetch.' And don't kid yourself. Your phone will start to ring the minute I hit the city limits. And you know it."

Joan smiled, looked at me, and pointed to where she had thrown the stick. "Speed. Fetch!"

Fetch wasn't a word I knew, but I knew what Joan wanted me to do, so I obediently went after the stick with little enthusiasm. I knew Babe wanted me to play the game, so I did. I dropped the missile at Joan's feet, which brought smiles from both.

Joan looked down at Speed and then back to Babe. "And what about this guy? What's going to happen to him?"

Babe was thoughtful for a few minutes, then said, "That's something I wanted to talk to you about."

"Oh. And what does that mean?"

"I want you to have him."

"Me? Um, I'm not so sure about that, Babe. Are you serious?"

"Yes. You and Speed mean more than anything to me. I love you both very much. It makes perfect sense that I give him to you. My folks can't take him, and I don't want to give him to anyone else. It would be a great honor if you would take him. He would not be a problem, and I think your dad would warm up to him quickly."

I was still sitting at Joan's feet, waiting for her to do something with the stick I had returned to her. She noticed finally and bent down to give me loving pats on my head. Then she straightened up and said, "It might be fine, Babe. Let me talk to my folks and see what they think, okay?"

Babe pulled Joan back into his arms, lovingly caressed her hair, and kissed her. "I love you, Joan. If you take Speed, I'll have one more reason to return to Barrymore."

Joan looked at Babe, "I love you too, Babe. Now, we'd better get to your house, or we'll be in trouble with your mom."

"Yeah, I guess we don't want to mess up Mom's schedule today, do we?"

When we arrived at the house, Babe held the front door open for Joan. As Dad greeted us inside the living room, I slipped in ahead of everybody.

"You kids have a seat. I'll go see how I can help Mom." With that, Dad stepped into the dining room and disappeared through the door into the kitchen.

Babe and Joan sat on the big over-stuffed sofa in the living room. I sat down at Babe's feet. Babe turned to Joan. "Well, good, we can continue talking. "Joan kicked off her shoes, tucked her legs underneath her body, and smiled at Babe. "Okay, what would you like to talk about?"

"What we were talking about before. You know, us. And did I mention I was not crazy about you dating other guys?"

"So, you are telling me I can't do that? Really?"

Babe paused for a few moments, then said. "No, I guess I can't say that. It's just hard for me to think about it."

"Then don't think about it, Babe. Let's enjoy our time and leave the rest to the Lord to deal with, like we talked about, okay?" She reached over and tapped Babe on the knee. "By the way, I noticed you were taking copious notes in church this morning."

"Yeah, well, I was struck by what Pastor Kieffer was talking about."

"Like what?"

"What he was teaching about the wide and narrow gates."

"What about it?"

Babe became cynical. "Yeah, I thought so. You weren't listening, were you?"

"Probably not as close as you were."

"Okay, listen up. What Mr. Kieffer said is important! According to the Gospel of Matthew, there are two roads—one that leads to eternal life and one to eternal death. Did you understand that?"

"Yes, well, pretty much. So how do you know you are on the right road?"

"That's a great question, Joan. Let me find that passage." Babe reached over to a small end table and grabbed his Bible from where he had laid it. He quickly flipped through the pages until he found what he wanted.

"Here it is in Matthew 7. Remember Joan; this is Jesus Himself talking here. He says, 'Enter through the narrow gate; for the gate is wide and the way broad that leads to destruction, and there are many who enter through it. For the gate is small and the way narrow that leads to life, and there are few who find it.'" Babe paused for a moment and looked at Joan. "It is saying that there are only two roads: the road to eternal life, heaven, and the road to eternal death, which is hell. And most people are on the road that leads to hell? Wow! That is amazing to me. So, this tells us we need to look for the narrow path. And that most people are on the wide path and therefore going in the wrong direction."

"Yes, we have always known there is only one way to heaven. But to most people, that sounds mean and narrow-minded," Joan replied. "At least, it seems that way to me."

Babe responded, "Maybe, but think of it this way. Most people believe they can get to heaven by being good, helping others, not cussing, and attending church. But according to the Bible, salvation is by God's grace: not what we do, but what He did on the cross."

Babe quickly flipped forward in his Bible. "Here it is, Ephesians 2. 'For by grace you have been saved through faith; and that not of yourselves, it is the gift of God; not because of works, so that no one may boast.'"

"Sounds pretty simple, but still---"

"But still, what?"

"It seems like you need to be doing something, like good deeds and stuff."

"That's right, but good deeds come naturally once you've come to Christ. If you got to heaven by doing good works, your salvation would be all about you and what you did. Getting to heaven is about what Jesus did: dying on the cross and coming out of the grave three days later. If it were about us and our good works, we would all be full of pride. The Bible says God hates pride. We can't earn our way to heaven by good deeds. No, we get to heaven through God's grace."

CHAPTER 15

HE'S JUST A DOG, AFTER ALL

With everyone seated around the large dining room table and heads bowed, Dad asked for God's blessing on the meal and the family. He thanked the Lord for Joan's presence, the morning service, and the beautiful day.

When he finished praying, everyone said, "Amen."

Mom said, "Babe, pass the veggies to Joan, and let's dig in while everything is hot." Hot meals were important to Mom. To me, hot meals don't matter that much.

The dinner Mom had prepared that day was a family favorite—an English roast with mashed potatoes, asparagus, and Yorkshire pudding. It was fine dining, and I expected to get a good share of the leftovers. The problem with formal dinners was that they always dragged on, and I had to wait for my turn to eat. Most of the time, I would sit or lie near where Babe sat, but this time I decided to lie down behind Mom's chair. I could have chosen any place to lie down, and that seemed to be the spot for me that day.

Dinner did last a very long time—lots of talking and eating. I couldn't wait until they stopped talking so I could start eating. I looked up a few times and wagged my tail, but no one noticed. They were having a good time. No one paid any attention to me.

At long last, the talking finally slowed down. Mom stood and picked up some dishes. Joan, who wanted to do the right thing, stood up to help Mom. Mom took a step back from the table. Unfortunately, she was unaware that I was there and fell backward over me. When Mom went down, immediate chaos erupted. Everything in her arms came crashing to the floor, breaking plates, scattering food, and sending eating utensils flying across the dining room floor. To make bad things even worse, when Joan stepped over to give Mom a hand, her foot slipped in the mashed potatoes, and she immediately joined Mom on the floor.

I dodged away momentarily, but I had learned long ago that floor food was my food. So, I dug in. Mashed potatoes, gravy, leftover roast beef, and buttered rolls were a wall-to-wall feast, and I didn't waste any time staking my rightful claim.

Babe and Dad jumped up and rushed over to help the ladies get back on their feet.

"Are you okay? Are you hurt?" both men asked as they grabbed for up-reaching arms. The ladies, with difficulty, steadied themselves and stood. Once they were stable, they began to brush away clinging dinner fragments, which I also immediately scooped up once they hit the floor.

"I'm fine," they both replied. They turned to one another to brush the food away.

Everyone's attention turned to Joan as tears accumulated in the corners of her eyes.

"Oh, dear," Mom said, embracing Joan and patting her softly. "It's okay, dear. No harm done."

"I'm so sorry," she whispered.

"It's no problem, Joan," Mom said as she held her close. "That darn dog is always underfoot, it seems."

"I'm fine," Joan uttered as she looked at Babe, who did nothing to help either lady. Joan was embarrassed. She steadied herself by placing her hand against the back of the chair, looked at Babe, and said, "I probably should be getting home."

Babe immediately responded to this suggestion with a frown. "Are you sure you're okay?" He drew close to her and put his hand on her shoulder.

"I'm okay, Babe," Joan replied shakily. "I've had a great time, but it's time to go."

Babe, clearly disappointed, said, "I'm so sorry about my dog."

"Well, it's not his fault. He is just a dog, after all."

Babe frowned and started to respond but checked himself.

Dad, who had been quiet, walked over and looked down at me. He was stern-faced and visibly upset. In a harsh tone, he said, "Get outside where you belong, Speed! You tripped my wife. That's unforgivable. Get outside. Now!" Dad stomped through the kitchen to the back door.

"Come on!" He glared at me as I slinked past him through the door he was holding open. His final words to me were, "You're a bad dog!" He slammed the door, and I was outside, "where I belonged."

To my surprise and disappointment, Babe did not come to my defense. However, I've long since forgiven him for that. Babe respected his dad and was intimidated by him as well. To say I was devastated would be a classic understatement. I had caused Mom embarrassment and pain. It was an accident, but I probably shouldn't have been lying there. I felt terrible. My heart was so heavy I felt sick to my stomach. What could I do to make up for this trouble I had caused?

I headed to the front porch, always my refuge. But there was no refuge there today. It felt awful being once again alone and rejected. The loneliness of years long past came to mind. I had experienced abandonment before, but I had never known the emptiness of family abandonment. I knew I needed time to think things over for a while, so I jumped to the ground and took off at a steady trot with no destination in mind. I just needed to get out of the neighborhood.

I meandered through town and headed south until I found myself at my former home on Hogsback. I sat on the bluff and tried to clear my mind, which proved impossible to do.

Does Babe hate me now? Why didn't he defend me? Does he think I'm a mutt?

I couldn't answer those questions and soon realized Hogsback was not where I needed to be. This hill was my old life. Like the porch, it was not a refuge for me that day either. So, I came down off Hogsback and headed back to town. In a few minutes, I was again in front of my home. The house was quiet and looked empty. The car was gone.

Were they out searching for me?

How do you deal with being kicked out of your home? I didn't know what to do. I felt ashamed of what had happened. I wanted forgiveness. I wanted my master, but I was not sure he wanted me. I needed a friend.

* * *

It was dark when I arrived at the front yard of Kate's house. I made my way around to the back, and much to my relief, she was there, snuggled down on a soft rug on the back porch. When she sensed my presence, she sat up and thumped her beautiful tail on the porch floor to greet me. We kissed and then scampered down the steps and onto the grassy yard, where we enjoyed high-spirited play for several minutes. That was so much fun, and it made me forget for a few minutes the trouble I had just left.

Kate still excited me. We sent love messages back and forth as we acted out our aggressions toward one another. After we made several trips around the yard gnawing on and mauling one another, we were ready for a break. I went over to Kate's water dish and started lapping up the contents, and of course, I was joined immediately by Kate.

"Get out of here, little girl," I growled.

Kate whimpered, "I love you." Then she pushed me aside and started lapping up the water supply. I moved over to a shaded spot on the grass and lay down.

As I lay there watching Kate drink from her bowl of water, my mind drifted back to Big and how close we were, and how dear Kate had become to me. We were friends and always would be, but I knew there was no comparison between my relationship with her and my relationship with my master. Not having Babe in my life was unthinkable. And the horror of the thoughts of being kicked out of Babe's house, and maybe his life, was more than I could stand.

Kate wandered over and lay down near me. We were face to face, just eyeballing one another. There were no puppies left in our family. There had been no problem finding homes for all the pups. Mr. Greer, the state trooper, kept one for himself. He wanted to train him to work in a K9 unit for the Oregon State Police Department. Mr. Greer named him "Blue" for the Blue Mountain Range in the area. It may have also been because of the blue uniform he wore. He got a good dog who would be a solid young four-legged trooper by now.

As a dad, I missed them, of course, but it didn't bother me because that is how families are in a dog's world. There is love and friendship, but long-term relationships within a dog's family are unusual. Only the relationship a dog has with his master is permanent.

While I lay looking at Kate, I noticed a familiar sight, a large bird soaring overhead. He swerved toward the two of us and then back up again, gently landing on the top of a medium-sized pine tree.

I recognized this magnificent bird the minute he flew over us. It was Hootie, faithful Hootie, who always seemed to show up whenever I was at a crossroads. As was my custom whenever Hootie landed nearby, I went straight over to the base of the tree he was on and put my front legs up on the trunk, greeting him with friendly barks. He returned the greeting with a cacophony of hoots. I remember how I wanted to be able to climb up that tree and share his tree limb so I could soak up some of Hootie's wisdom. He knew that. I could tell by how he looked at me through his large, scholarly eyes.

"Your family is grieving for you, lad. Return to your master. Your life is in him. There is no other." Our eyes locked for several minutes. Hootie was statuesque, like a king on his throne dishing out pearls of wisdom— wisdom I needed to hear. I held my position, standing on two legs and staring into Hootie's huge, yellow eyes.

Then suddenly, as if guided by an unseen power, Hootie spread his massive wings and launched himself from the tree. He circled over us once as he reached cruising altitude and headed south toward town. At that minute, I knew I had to decide. Yes, I could return to my old ways of wandering and living independently. Or I could stay here if I wanted to. I was sure Kate's family would not mind having another dog around. But that wouldn't work either. There was only one choice for me. I needed Babe, and I knew that Babe wanted me. I had to get back to my master's house. It was settled.

The following morning, just as the sun broke over the eastern mountain range, I said goodbye to Kate and headed for Barrymore, a short distance to the south. It was a clear and warm late August morning. As I trotted along, a sweet morning breeze filled my nostrils with the aroma of fresh-cut hay. The air teemed with the scents of a vast array of late-blooming wildflowers, alpine fir trees, and whirring hummingbirds. Their little bodies darted in and out of nearby gullies filled with pussy willows and hollyhocks. These sights and sounds cheered me and intensified my excitement to get home to Babe, and I felt good about things. My depression was gone. I was heading home.

Farm animals were grazing nearby. They paused and looked up when they saw a strange animal trespassing across their land. I was traveling through a field of tall prairie grass, but I could see the gravel road I needed straight ahead, less than fifty yards away. I was excited, knowing I would be with my family soon. Whatever it took, we would always be together.

With that thought, my pace quickened. I could picture myself jumping into Babe's arms again, just like when he came home from family vacation, which seemed so long ago. We would fall to the ground together and roll around, loving one another as we had done many times.

I was halfway to the gravel road when I heard a blast from a gunshot and felt a sharp pain slam into my back right leg, causing my hindquarters to crumble and throw me to the ground. I had no immediate idea what had happened, but I no longer had control of my leg, which was bleeding profusely. I began nursing the wound with my tongue in a frantic effort to stop the bleeding.

CHAPTER 16
TIME OUT

s I lay nursing my wound with my tongue, my thoughts flashed back to the caretaker of the city dump and when he had pursued a wounded Big through stashes of junk until he found him and killed him.

Was this going to happen to me? Was a shooter now coming after me? I need to get away from here!

I forced myself to crawl along the ground toward the road. It was painful, but I finally reached the fence. I scrunched underneath it and into a shallow gulley that ran alongside the road. The blood from my wound began to flow again, so I lay in the ditch for a long time, nursing the injury until the bleeding stopped.

I'm unsure how long I lay in the ditch, but it seemed endless. An occasional vehicle passed by, but no one noticed me. Fortunately, whoever shot me didn't seem to be looking for me. I knew I needed help, but I was too weak to pull myself out of the ditch and onto the road. All I could do to attract attention was to yelp when I heard a car coming, but the noise the vehicles made on the gravel road drowned out my yelps. As the afternoon wore on, my cries for help became weak and futile.

Dusk began to settle in when at last, I heard voices of people coming toward me as they walked alongside the road. A couple out for an evening stroll triggered new hope. They were headed straight for me.

They must see me! Hurry, folks. I'm right in front of you. I'll let you know. I'll bark when you're close. Please listen.

They couldn't get there fast enough as far as I was concerned. When they got close, I uttered a pitiful cry that caught their attention; it even startled them. However, it didn't take them long to recover. They hurried over and knelt beside me.

The man quickly looked me over and said, "He's been shot." He visually examined my wound while at the same time softly stroking my head.

"Why would someone do that?" the lady offered. "Such a pretty dog."

"We need to get him to a vet," the man said. "But we need to move fast. I'm sure he's lost a ton of blood."

"The vet is twenty-five miles away," she replied. "They may be closed by now."

"You stay here with him, and I'll run to the house and see if I can get a hold of them."

"Okay, but hurry, Eddy. He looks like he may be fading."

The man jumped to his feet and took off on a dead run in the direction they had come from as the lady sat down and eased my head into her lap.

"There you are, little man," she said, softly patting my head. "You're going to be just fine. At least you are wearing a tag, so they should be able to locate your owner. I'm sure your family will be glad to get you back."

As she sat there cradling my head in her arms, I felt my body relax. I was exhausted, and my leg hurt badly, but somehow, I knew I would be okay. They would get me to Babe. I knew that for sure. Then all would be fine once again.

In a few minutes, a car pulled up, and Eddy got out. He opened the back door on the passenger side and hurried over to where we were. I wasn't sure how, but they managed to get me into the back seat of their sedan without killing me. I was glad about that, of course. Eddie had put a clean sheet over everything in the back of the car, and he eased me inside and covered me with the sheet. Then they jumped into the front seat and sped off for LaGrange, Oregon.

I must have dozed off because the next thing I knew, I was being lifted out of the back of the car by a strange man, who carried me into a building and laid me out on a metal table.

"What happened to you, laddie?"

A strange voice. I lifted my head to see who was speaking.

"Did you get after some farmer's chickens or something?" He asked these questions while holding me down and gently stroking my neck. At that point, a younger man moved up to the table. I learned later I was being attended to by an animal doctor and his son, who was training to become a veterinarian.

"Let me look at your leg and see if I can amputate it." Then he chuckled and said, "Just kidding about that, buddy."

As his son held me down, the vet leaned in and closely examined my leg wound. Then he cleaned the area with a soapy solution from a bowl while gently spraying the damage with water from a small rubber hose.

None of this felt very good, but the trainee held me so firmly that I could do nothing about it. He kept a line of gab going through the procedure, saying things like, "I got you, boy. You're going to be fine. Are you hungry, boy? We'll get you something to eat after I get through abusing you. How does that sound?"

Then the young man looked at his dad, who had quietly examined every part of my leg and hind quarters. "How does it look, Pop?"

The vet leaned back so the son could see the wound.

"Take a look. The bullet passed on through. You can see some muscle and tendon damage, but this will heal over time. Get an antibiotic in him, and then we'll attach a stabilizer and shave and wrap the leg. He should be able to hobble on his own in a few days."

Then he paused a few seconds and continued speaking to me. "So, the question is, who will pay your vet bill, laddie? You'd better have an owner show up who will cover your medical expenses, plus room and board. The lovely people who brought you in gave me thirty bucks, but that won't do it. Not with my rates, anyway. You'll owe me five hundred bucks before you get out of here. How are you going to handle that, laddie? You'd better have a rich owner. Otherwise, laddie, my boy, you'll be around here a long time. A very long time."

The vet grinned and started patting my head. "Oh well, don't worry about it, laddie. I'm sure it's going to be okay. We'll have your tag checked tomorrow morning. I'm guessing you have an anxious owner who wants you back."

I lay there quietly while the vet carefully wrapped my leg with soft cotton padding around the stabilizer bar and secured it with strips of stretch tape.

The trainee brought out a stiff plastic cone at that moment, and the vet put it over my head. "You're not going to like this," he said. "But we don't want you digging at that wound.

Don't fret," he continued. "You'll feel better in a couple of days and be moving around on your own in no time." Then they transferred me to a small table with wheels. The young trainee guided me to an open cage and, with care, placed me inside. There was a soft cushion, a fresh water bowl, and another bowl with food inside. I was glad to see both but had difficulty getting to them without putting weight on my right side. It was a little messy, but I managed to get it done.

"Good night," the young man said as he stroked my neck. "Tomorrow, if you are up to it, I'll take you around and introduce you to some of our other guests.

We have some interesting characters around here. See you tomorrow, buddy."

That night was long. I was in pain, and I now realize it would have been even worse if they hadn't given me a shot containing a pain sedative. Despite the drugs, I lay awake most of the night, wondering how to get out of this place and find my way back to my family. I knew Babe would be looking for me. Despite what I had done, I knew he loved me and would forgive me.

But how would he find me? And how would I find him?

The following day I was awakened by barking coming from another room. There seemed to be at least two dogs involved. My room was quiet, but soon I could hear a human talking to the dogs and knew they were okay because of the aroma of food and the fact that they had quieted down. The vet's son was in front of my cage a few minutes later, holding a bowl of food.

Wonderful!

"Here you go, boy. How are you feeling this morning?" He gave me soft pats on my head and set the bowl before my nose. "You eat this, and I'll be back with some more later. Meanwhile, we'll let your family know you are here with us. How does that sound?" He reached in and stroked my head for a few minutes. I felt his love.

"Goodbye, buddy. I'd love to stay, but I have other customers to look after. I'll be back, okay?"

The trainee departed, and it was quiet except for an occasional bark. I was alone and left to my thoughts. As always, they began with my master, Babe.

When will I see him again? Is he looking for me? Does he still love me, even though I had made a mess of things when we had dinner as a family? I wanted to see him again so badly, to hear his voice, to feel his hand on my neck and head. *When I see him again, I'll jump into his arms and kiss his face a thousand times. Well, on second thought, I won't be able to jump into his arms right away, but he'll understand. He understands everything.*

How long will they keep me here? If Babe doesn't come for me soon, I'm out of here the first chance I get. I may be unable to jump through one of these windows, but if they start walking me outside, it's goodbye, Speed! All they will see is the fur on the back of my tail waving a fond goodbye, bad leg and all. I'll be finding my master. That happy thought made me feel a lot better.

I must have dozed off for a while after that. The next thing I heard was the sound of my unlocked cage door and the young man's voice.

"Hey, boy, a visitor in the lobby named Babe is asking about you. Do you know him?

Babe? Did he say, Babe? That's my master's name.

My tail started to wag. I could feel my entire body begin to tremble.

"So, you do know him. Well, he's here, in the lobby. He's come to pick you up, Speed. That's your name. Let me get you out of your cage and onto this gurney, okay?"

He carefully lifted me out of the cage and onto the gurney. He then started to roll me toward a large door.

"Okay, we will go through this door, but I need you to stay on the gurney, okay? You'll be excited to see your owner, but you must stay on the gurney, okay, Speed? Stay on the gurney! If you try to jump off, I may need to be mean to you. Do you understand, Speed?"

I didn't understand, but as excited as I was to see Babe, I knew one thing—I would need to stay on the gurney.

The minute we went through the door, I caught the scent of my master. My tail began to thump against the cushion on which I was lying. I started to tremble. Then, I heard Babe speak, and my body lurched forward. The intern immediately stopped and held me on the cart.

Babe came into view. "Hey buddy, it's okay. I'm right here." He patted my head, back, side, and three good legs. I was covering his hand and arm with kisses. We continued those greetings to one another for several minutes until I relaxed, and my heart toned down to a regular beat. After that, we made a short trip out to the car, and Babe picked me up and put me in the front seat, my usual place in the family car.

The trip from LaGrange to Barrymore went quickly because I had received a drug before we left the vet's office and slept the whole time.

That night, Mom cooked up a special dinner of English stew with plenty of meat, especially in my dish. I received much attention, including a large bowl of ice cream for dessert. We were a loving family once again. It was indeed a little bit of heaven on earth. I expected it would last forever. There was no reason to think it would ever change.

Because my leg was in a soft cast, Babe prepared a bed for me next to the lower bunk. Den was not home that summer, as he was doing a science internship in

Germany. Babe got into bed and propped his head up so we could see one another.

"I thank God we found you, Speed. We were all worried that we might have lost you forever. You are so important to our family, more than you realize. We all feel terrible about how we treated you. It was not your fault the accident happened, yet you took the blame. I'm sorry, Speed. Will you forgive me, buddy?"

Babe reached out and stroked my head and neck. I licked his hand.

I was overwhelmed by the love I felt for Babe that night. I was delighted to be back with my family. I was happy. *Everything is back to what it once was. There will be no more separation. I'll never let Babe out of my sight again.*

Unfortunately, that was untrue.

Babe and I were so close, I could tell when Babe was uncomfortable with what he was telling me. This was the case when he said to me one day, "You know, Speed, I'm going to leave for college in a month. I won't be here to take care of you once that happens. So, I want you to know I've arranged for you to live with Joan out on her farm for the time I'm gone. She is excited about having you, and I promise she will take good care of you when

I'm gone. Your leg should heal before I leave. And I think you can help her dad on the farm. I told him you are a farm collie and could help him around the farm. He has some cows and a couple of horses. So, you will fit right in there with your herding instincts. What do you think, Speed? Would you be willing to give it a try? It would make me feel good if you and Joan were together while I'm gone."

I gave Babe a look of uncertainty. He roughed up my neck and patted my head. "You'll be fine, Speed. I'll do my best to get back here as often as possible. You and Joan are my two best friends. I love you both. After college, we'll spend the rest of our lives together. Okay, Speed?"

CHAPTER 17
A NEW ADDRESS

When I was on Earth, I would have done anything my master asked me to do, even die for him if necessary. I am very sure we all would have handled the final days of our last summer together much differently if we could do them over again.

No one considered my feelings in the vital decisions made that summer, even though I was a bona fide family member. Many of those family discussions were about me. I realize I was a junior member of the family, "just a dog, after all." However, the term "family" should include everyone in the house, should it not? I had always been considered and treated as a family member. We all had our roles to play, whether human or animal. A family comprises creatures brought together by God to love and help one another. And that's the critical part—we deal with each other's needs. Well, what about my needs? I realize now that their decision was probably the only one they could have made. But I couldn't understand it then.

Be that as it may, one day in early September, Babe came out of the house and called me to the car. He gave me a long and loving hug and several head pats. Then he said, "Are you ready to go for a ride, pal?"

Well, I understood those words. They were always welcome. Any trip with Babe was a treat as far as I was concerned. Babe opened the front passenger door to the family car, and I climbed in. Babe got in, and we were on our way. To where? It didn't matter to me. Anywhere with Babe was fine.

Babe drove us down Alder Street, made a left turn onto Main Street, and headed out of town, eastbound, to an area known as Cricket Flat. We were on our way to the small farmhouse where Joan lived. There was a lot to see as I gazed out my window, which Babe had cranked down for me once we were underway. We passed farm buildings, cows and horses grazing in open pastures, a river, a canyon, Horseshoe Bend, logging trucks heading for local sawmills, and little animals hurrying from one side of the highway to the other without getting hit by a vehicle.

When we arrived, Babe pulled the car onto the gravel driveway next to Joan's house. A separate two-car garage was at the end of the driveway, and a family home was on the left. There was a large fenced-in yard around three sides of the house. Beyond that, to the south, stood a large red barn and several metal buildings where Joan's dad stored his tractors and farm implements.

Babe got out of the car and came around to my side. He opened the door, and I hopped out. A strange and unexplainable weak feeling suddenly overcame me, and I sidled up to Babe's legs and sat. Joan came out of the house in a few minutes, followed by her parents. They shared a short visit and then walked over to some yard furniture at the back of the house, where they sat and visited some more.

I lay down at Babe's feet and put my head on his shoe closest to our car. I didn't know why, but I felt uneasy about this little get-together. Joan's mom entered the house and returned with a tray full of iced drinks, which she served to everyone. Of course, nothing was for me, but that was a small matter. Something was up. I grew anxious to get out of there.

After about an hour, Babe stood and said goodbye to everyone, which was great because I was ready to go. I followed him to the car, but he kneeled and hugged me instead of opening the door. He started talking to me very softly and lovingly.

"I love you, Speed," he said. "You have been my faithful friend for a long time. You will always be my dog. But I can't keep you now, Speed. I must give you up because I'm going away to college." His voice became hoarse. "I can't take you back with me, Speed. I'm sorry, buddy."

He paused and cleared his throat, choking back a soft sob. "I'm giving you to Joan, Speed. You can live here and be part of her family now. She has promised to care of you and love you just like I love you, Speed. I'm sorry, but it must be this way."

I didn't know what Babe said, but I could see and feel his emotion. I pushed my nose up to his face and kissed him.

It's okay. Now let's get in the car and go home.

"Stay, Speed," he said as he stood up.

Stay, Speed? Are you kidding me?

Of course, I knew what that meant. I obeyed whenever Babe told me to stay because I knew he would always release me from that command when he was ready. But this time, as he was talking, he opened the car door, retrieved a short lead rope from the car, and snapped it onto my neck chain. He then handed the lead to Joan, who had joined us on the driveway.

My mind began to race. I felt a surge of panic twist its way through my body.

What is going on here?

I couldn't understand what my master was saying or doing. Multiplying my confusion, Babe then turned away, jumped into the car, and drove away without looking back.

Where was Babe going without me? Is he coming back? Of course, he's coming back. Babe would never leave me!

So, I waited. I had no choice. Joan had attached my lead to a rope secured to a tree in the front yard. Not necessary. I would have stayed anyway because Babe told me to stay. I locked my eyes on every vehicle coming from the west. There were many, but none was the right one. I kept waiting and watching. During the evening, Joan exited the house several times to pat and talk to me.

She said a lot to encourage me that night. "You're going to like it here, Speed. I'll get my horse, Dusty, out of the barn, and we'll take some rides together. There are a lot of neat places we can explore together. My dad will make you a place to stay in one of his sheds or maybe on the back porch."

She even brought me a plate of food from their dinner table. She wanted to make me feel at home, but I didn't feel much like eating. I was looking for Babe to show up and needed to be the first to see and greet him. He was my master, and he would be coming back to get me and take me home.

So, I waited and waited. I stayed there all night. But Babe didn't come back to get me. When morning dawned, I was still there. Traffic began to pick up, and I felt some renewed excitement. Babe must have needed to spend the night away for some reason. Now he would soon be back to pick me up. I was ready—more than ready.

Joan and her family came and went throughout the day. One of them would stop and talk to me, pat me, and then go on their way. Joan came by several times, which I appreciated, but I tried not to be distracted from my watch. I knew Babe would be driving the next car over the hill.

Come on, Babe. I know you're on your way. Get here. Be the next car. Please!

But Babe was not the next car, the next car after that, or the dozens of vehicles that followed. By late afternoon, it finally dawned on me.

Babe is not coming back. That's what he had been trying to tell me. He had given me to Joan. But Joan's not my master. Babe is. I don't want another master.

I lay down and put my head between my paws. The traffic kept coming, mostly farm trucks, hay balers, and slow-moving tractors looking for a field to work in or a shed in which to park. I saw cars and logging trucks speeding by with purpose, all with destinations. I had no purpose or destination. I was going nowhere. I was just a dog tied to a tree, and once again, my status was "mutt." A mutt tied to a tree, no less. No one wanted me, not even Babe.

Not even Babe!? After what we had been through together? No way was I going to believe that. Babe loved me. He told me we would always be together, and Babe would never lie to me.

CHAPTER 18
GOING HOME

By mid-afternoon, I had decided to go home. I didn't know what the problem was, but I knew there had to be one.

Was Babe hurt? Or have I done something to cause him not to want me anymore?

I didn't know what to think, but if I was going to find him, I had to go home and start from there. I felt terrible because I knew I had disobeyed my master, who had told me to stay there, but living without Babe was unacceptable. I had no choice. I had to go home and find Babe.

As she had done many times throughout my two days there, Joan came out to comfort me. She had undoubtedly heard my whining. I had been making noise all afternoon, whimpering and crying out for Babe and continually pacing back and forth as far as the rope would let me. Joan knelt beside me and put her arm around me.

"You're feeling it, aren't you, boy? I know. I miss him too, Speed. He wanted me to have you as a symbol of his great love for us. I tried telling him you wouldn't be happy here, but he wouldn't listen."

She cradled my head and looked at me with determined eyes. "We need to make a go of this, Speed. We can do it! We have no choice. I promised Babe. I can't just let you go. If I did, you would take off for home, and Babe isn't even there, Speed. He's away at college. And his folks will be moving to the coast any day now."

Joan paused momentarily and turned my head, so we were eye to eye. "Honestly, I think you'll begin to like it here in a few weeks. My dad could use you. We're your family now."

She patted my head and said, "We've got to make it work, Speed. For Babe's sake."

Her tear-wet eyes drifted to the western skyline, which had blossomed into a beautiful sunset. "I wish I could change things for you, Speed, but I can't."

As darkness settled in for the night, I began chewing on the rope attached to my chain collar. It took several hours to chew it in two, but I got the job done and was free to leave, which I did, heading westward into the night to find my master.

As I ran along, I tried to stay to the side of the road to avoid the traffic, but the gravel there was loose and sharp and soon began to hurt my feet. To combat this, I moved onto the pavement and tried to stay close to the edge. When I heard traffic approaching from behind me, I quickly darted from the pavement to avoid getting hit. I began to feel tinges of pain in my bad leg occasionally, but nothing I couldn't handle.

I made good time for a long while. As time went on, however, I felt increasing pain in my injured leg, and running became more difficult. Most of the traffic consisted of large trucks, which were very loud and scared me to the side of the road each time they blew by me. I had to employ last-minute evasive tactics several times, and the quick dodging and darting began to take a toll on my right rear leg.

The truth is, there was no safe place for me on that highway that night. I should have waited until daylight and stuck to the side of the road, but I didn't do either of those two things. I was going home. Nothing was going to stop me.

It was long and painful after that, but I rejoiced when a familiar sight loomed ahead—Horseshoe Bend, named because it was the point where the road made a one-hundred-and-eighty degree turn before it straightened out and swung back to the west. From there, it would be all downhill with immediate entry into Barrymore. Babe and I had driven to Horseshoe Bend several times because of a side road detour from which we could pull off and move to an overlook. We would leave the car and gaze down at our town of Barrymore, nestled in the beautiful Grande Ronde Valley. This viewing point was one of our favorite places in the world. I cherished those memories.

But now I was on a mission. A mission to find my master. And I was moving slowly.

Will Babe be there when I got home?

The strange things that had happened in those past days made me wonder. There had been many phone calls and visitors, mostly Babe's friends from school. And there were those darn suitcases. They always meant bad news. The same thing happened when Den went away. Lots of activity, and then Den was gone.

Is this going to be a repeat of that?

Right then, I heard a familiar "hoot" coming from the rock crest above me as I approached Horseshoe Bend. I spotted my old friend Hootie sitting high up on the rock shelf that overlooked the bend in the road.

Welcome sounds of "hoot, hoot" filled the air, but all I could do was look up at him and then put my head down and keep moving. I hated to ignore Hootie, but my concentration had to be on the next step ahead.

"Hoot," came again and again. Hootie was trying to tell me something, but I didn't care. I was tired and almost home. I loved Hootie, but this was not a good time.

Sorry, Hootie. I'll catch up with you later, friend.

When I came out of the turn, the bright lights of my hometown blinked as if encouraging me to stay the course. Thankfully, the amount of traffic had decreased as truckers began to pull into rest areas along the way. I could see the baseball field lights to the south of town. Babe wasn't playing summer ball, but chances were good he would be at the game. It would be another place to look if I didn't find him at home.

Despite the pain, my pace picked up, and I thought of seeing my master soon. The pain seemed to diminish proportionally to the closing distance to town. I crossed over to the right side of the highway. The bridge over the Grand Ronde River loomed ahead. This bridge was on the east end of town, and my home was not far from the bridge. I could hear the water surge against the riverbanks. How good it would be to drink my thirst away from the freshwater of a beautiful river.

Then out of the darkness, I heard a familiar sound. "YOWRL."

Fergie? Could it be? It must be. Who else makes a sound like that?

"Fergie?" I barked.

Another "YOWRL" came from across the highway. Then I spotted her. She was standing in front of a small storage shed, one of the rest area buildings.

I crossed back over the highway and trotted over to greet my former adversary. To my surprise, Fergie stepped from the shadows and greeted me by rubbing up against my legs, a rare tender moment between us.

"Fergie, where have you been? I've been looking all over for you."

"A human grabbed me off the street one day and brought me over here. That's all I know. But he was a dumb human, so he couldn't hold on to me very long."

"That doesn't surprise me,"

"What are you doing over here? How's Babe?"

"Long story," I replied. "Come on. I'll tell you on the way home. But first, I've got to have a drink of water."

Once again, I crossed over the highway with Fergie following me closely. We went down to the river's edge, where the water was calm, and took in enough of the good-tasting water to sustain us for the rest of the trip. When we had our fill, I led us back across the highway one more time. We then made our way to the far edge of the highway and proceeded toward town. Bright lights and fan noise from the baseball stadium seemed to be calling out to me.

Why not? I could run over and check for Babe there because there was a good chance he or Dad would be at the game. And if not, we'd head for home. However, that would mean crossing two lanes of traffic with Fergie in tow, and the highway was quite busy. That sounded like a bad idea.

I turned to Fergie. "You wait here while I go check out the stadium, okay?"

In reply, Fergie purred something. I couldn't tell what. "Fergie, wait here. I'll be right back!" And I started across the highway. When I reached the median, I stopped and looked back at Fergie. Unfortunately, she had misunderstood my directions and started to follow me across the eastbound lanes.

"No, Fergie. Get back," I barked. Obviously confused, Fergie stopped and looked up at me and stopped in the middle of the highway. At the same time, I saw a car heading toward her, which was quickly picking up speed as it headed out of town.

"Fergie, there's a car coming. Get back to the curb!!"

Fergie froze in place. She didn't know what to do. I came off the median at full speed and reached her just in time to knock her back toward the curb. There was a whine of skidding tires and screeching brakes. Everything went dark, followed by complete silence. The last thing I remember is seeing a vision of Babe and me. He had his fishing rod, and we were running toward the river. Babe was out of breath and calling out to me, "Slow down, Speed!"

EPILOGUE

It was my third night on campus. I was lying on a cot in my dorm room when a dorm mate knocked on my door. "You've got a phone call," he said when I opened the door. "It's just down the hall."

"Okay, thanks," I said and followed him down to one of the hall phones provided for the students.

"Hello."

"Son, this is Dad. How are you doing?"

"I'm doing fine, Dad. Uh, what's up?"

"Well, son, brace yourself. I have some terrible news."

My heart jumped. My first thought was that something had happened to Mom. I could feel a sudden surge of panic as a sickening feeling dumped a load of acid into my stomach. "What is it, Dad?"

"It's Speed. He's, uh, he's dead. He got hit by a car last night."

"Oh no. What happened?"

"I'm not sure, son. Joan's dad found him just east of town. He decided to come home, I guess. Allen said he went missing last night, so he went looking for him, and like I say, found him near the Grand Ronde River bridge."

I slid down the wall and sat on the floor. Tears streamed down my cheeks as I imagined the horror of that scene for my precious dog. Feelings of guilt, grief, and sickness overwhelmed me. My body trembled.

My immediate thought was, why had I been so stupid to think Speed would stay somewhere else?

That is a question I have asked myself hundreds of times since. Speed's loyalty to me far exceeded my loyalty to him. I had let him down. He was the most faithful friend I have ever had, and I failed him. How could I have been so careless?

I put the phone on the floor and blurted out, "Why, God? Why?"

As the years have passed, I've come to realize more and more the treasure of wisdom God gave me when he gave me Speed. Here is what I mean by that. When God gave me Speed, I became a master, his master, and he treated me as a servant would treat his master. Speed loved me beyond question and was willing to sacrifice himself for my well-being without question. He trusted me implicitly, even the times I let him down. He always forgave me, returning love in return for discipline or indifference on my part. Whatever I asked or told him to do, he quickly did. He slept with me in my bed. He was my best friend. One of my greatest blessings today is knowing my dog is in heaven. He is waiting for me to join him.

I have a Master too. My Master's name is Jesus Christ. And the model for my side of our relationship is my dog Speed. You see, I want to serve Jesus with the same attitude as this mere animal served me, "who was just a dog, after all." I want to love Jesus as Speed loved me. I want to be obedient as he was obedient, and faithful as he was faithful. When Speed woke up in the morning, I knew his first thoughts were of me, his master. Today, my first thoughts each morning are of my Master, Jesus.

Speed would always come and find me whenever we had been apart for any time. I was always in first place with him, no matter the circumstances. Speed belonged to an imperfect master. My Master is perfect. Yet, out of love, He submitted Himself to harsh treatment and death at the hands of men he had created.

On His last night with His disciples, He told them He was going to prepare a home in heaven for them and all the believers who came after them. He said, "If it were not true, I would have told you." I know He is waiting for me there.

God gave me Speed when I was a boy and needed a close friend. In His perfect timing, He took him away, along with everything else that was important to me as a child, replacing all those things with what was important to Him for the rest of time.

When I was a child, I used to speak like a child, think like a child, reason like a child; when I became a man, I did away with childish things.

—1 Corinthians 13:11